"Where are *you* planning on sleeping tonight, *Mrs. Sutherland?*"

Angie avoided her new husband's gaze and looked anxiously around the lavish bridal suite. "Well, this is a hotel.... There'll be other rooms available."

Owen's desire dissipated as his anger took over. "I won't have my wife going down to the front desk of a Sutherland hotel on her wedding night to request a separate room because she refuses to sleep with me."

Angie bit her lip. "I guess it would be embarrassing if people found out we didn't spend tonight together."

"Embarrassing? I'd be the laughingstock of the hotel, never mind the entire industry."

"Yes, we must maintain appearances, musn't we," she snapped. "After all, this is a *business* arrangement, not a marriage." Her eyes narrowed. "I'll take the couch."

"You will sleep on the damned bed," Owen said. "And so will I. We'll put a sword or something equally appropriate between us. Does that suit you, *Mrs. Sutherland?*"

"Perfectly," she retorted. So much for a wedding night to remember....

Jayne Ann Krentz has been a key contributor to the Temptation series since it launched in 1984. She has written twenty-two outstanding romances, each and every one close to her heart. Under the pen name Amanda Quick, this versatile writer has also had two historicals on the *New York Times* bestseller lists. Watch for Jayne's next Temptation, coming in January 1992. #377 *The Private Eye* is the first in an exciting twelve-book series called "Heroes."

The Wedding Night

JAYNE ANN KRENTZ

Harlequin Books

TORONTO • NEW YORK • LONDON
AMSTERDAM • PARIS • SYDNEY • HAMBURG
STOCKHOLM • ATHENS • TOKYO • MILAN

Published October 1991

ISBN 0-373-25465-2

THE WEDDING NIGHT

Printed in U.S.A.

1

THE VOLUMINOUS SATIN skirts of Angie Townsend's wedding gown sailed out behind her as her new husband took her hand and whisked her down the steps to the waiting limousine.

A shout went up and a hoard of Angie's laughing relatives charged on to the lawn to form a cheering gauntlet. It was easy to tell the Townsends from the rest of the multitude. Most of them had copper-tinted hair and eyes the color of a tropical sea, just as Angie did. They were all throwing themselves wholeheartedly into the festivities. It was the way the boisterous Townsend clan did things.

"I forgot about this part," Owen Sutherland muttered as he plunged into the crowd with Angie in tow.

Birdseed and flower petals descended like rain as the throng of well-wishers parted reluctantly to allow the bridal couple to pass. Several of the male guests offered racy advice about the wedding night, causing Angie to blush furiously.

"It's all your fault," she said to Owen. "If you'd wanted a quiet wedding you should never have put us Townsends in charge of things. We don't do things by halves."

"I can't say I wasn't warned," Owen admitted.

Angie turned to wave goodbye to her parents and her brother, Harry, who stood in the doorway of the elegant country club, glasses of champagne in their hands.

Angie's mother, one of the few non-redheads in the clan, was sobbing happily into a hankie. She had once confided to Angie that she had been quite restrained and proper in her younger days. Marrying a Townsend had ruined all her good breeding, she claimed.

Palmer Townsend, a robust, broad-shouldered man whose formal clothes did not quite conceal a small paunch, beamed at his daughter with paternal pride. He lifted the hand holding a champagne glass and toasted her as she was led toward the limousine.

Harry, at twenty-nine, three years older than Angie, merely grinned at her. He had his father's broad shoulders and strong build. He also still had plenty of the brilliant Townsend red hair, which had gone gray and somewhat thin on his father.

"The full production was worth the effort," Owen said. "You look like a fairy-tale princess in that gown." His crystal gray eyes slid over her in swift, satisfied appraisal as the uniformed limo driver stepped forward to open the car door.

Angie felt Owen's glance as though it were a living thing made of fire. Excitement bubbled inside her. There was something so incredibly vital about her husband, she thought. He was so intensely, overwhelmingly *male*. From his midnight black hair and hawklike features to his lean, solidly built body, he radiated a primitive masculine vitality.

The heat rose in Angie's cheeks as she saw the cool possessiveness in his eyes. Tonight Owen would be touching her even more intimately than he was now looking at her. Tonight he would make love to her for the first time. The thought took her breath away.

It was lack of opportunity, not lack of desire that had kept Angie out of her fiancé's bed until this point. Owen's incredibly busy schedule combined with the whirlwind nature of his courtship were the main reasons they had not yet made love. His arrogant insistence on not having his bride become the subject of tacky gossip in the local press or at the country club where he and Angie's father were both members had played a part, too. And of course, the overly protective, old-fashioned attitudes of the Townsend men had also been factors.

On top of everything else there had been a considerable amount of just plain bad timing, Angie decided regretfully. She had, after all, known Owen for only three months, and for the first two of those months she had been secretly terrified of him.

With a hunter's instincts Owen had wisely not pressed Angie into an intimate relationship. He had been content to court her gently, and in this manner, he'd drawn her into his force field with a sure hand.

He'd had a great deal of help from Angie's family, all of whom were delighted with the prospect of a marriage between Angie and Owen. As usual the members of the Townsend clan were convinced they knew what was best for Angie and took pains to tell her so.

Angie knew it was not just the fact that she was the youngest that made all the others adopt a paternalistic and protective attitude toward her. It had more to do with the fact that she was the only one in the family who had shown little interest in and even less aptitude for the family business, Townsend Resorts.

From an early age, Angie's interests had been in the realm of the artistic rather than the corporate world. This lack of flair for something everyone else in the family took for granted had given the rest of the Townsends the notion that Angie was naive by nature. As a result, the clan had gone out of its way to shelter Angie from the realities of big business. While her brother, Harry, was being groomed to take over his fathers position as head of the Townsend empire, Angie was encouraged to pursue her artistic endeavors.

Angie tolerated her family's indulgent attitude for the most part, only putting her foot down when someone went too far in trying to organize her life for her. But in the matter of Owen Sutherland, she had come to the conclusion that for once everyone was right. Owen Sutherland was the man for her.

It was during the past month that Angie had finally dared to admit to herself that she was enthralled by Owen. She had also come to the incredible realization that he genuinely needed and wanted her. But it seemed that after coming to that shattering conclusion, she had seen less of him than ever. Sudden, unexpected business demands had taken Owen out of Tucson for much of the time. When opportunities for privacy had presented themselves, she discovered her father or brother or mother was somehow in the way. Owen had not seemed to mind.

No one had been more surprised by her reaction to Owen Sutherland than Angie herself. Sutherland was not the kind of man she had envisioned marrying or becoming involved with. One look at him today, dressed in austere black and white formal attire, the sun revealing the hint of silver in his black hair, was enough to explain why. He was tall, dark and dangerous.

When Palmer Townsend had first introduced Owen to Angie, her initial impulse had been to run very fast in the opposite direction. Her reaction was not based on the knowledge that the Sutherlands had been business rivals of the Townsends for years. She cared little about the hotel business and considered the rivalry silly.

It was rather that she had taken one glimpse into the depths of Owen's unfathomable crystal eyes and known the man was going to be a serious problem. At that very first meeting Angie had been shaken by some secret, inner knowledge she could not explain. It was as if she had been existing in a world of sunlight, and now the Lord of the Underworld had come to carry her away with him.

That was before she had gotten to know him, of course—before she had come to understand the extent of Owen's need for her. Not that he had discussed that need the way a Townsend would have. Owen was a very private man, unaccustomed to voicing his emotions. Angie sensed that it might be a long while before her husband was able to discuss his feelings with her, but she was in love and fully prepared to wait.

Her new husband was a hard man in many ways and possessed of a formidable willpower and an iron-clad self-control. There was a natural arrogance about him that was not unlike that of her father and brother. It was the arrogance of men who were accustomed to leadership and power. But unlike the arrogance of her father and brother, Owen's arrogance had never been tempered with love.

No, Owen would never find it easy to admit he needed the gentleness of a woman in his life. But Angie knew he did. She was certain of it. Deep down inside Owen longed for the softness and intimacy she could give him. He needed a woman he could trust with his heart and soul. And Angie knew that Owen would never renege on a commitment—especially one as serious as marriage. In that respect he was very much like a Townsend.

Today Owen had stood in front of three hundred people and committed himself to Angie in no uncertain terms. *Until death do us part.* Shyly, but with all the determination of a woman in love, Angie had, in turn, promised herself to Owen Sutherland forever.

She had never been happier than she was at the moment Owen had slipped his ring on her finger. The smile she had given him had held her promise of love and faithfulness for a lifetime. Owen had looked deep into her eyes, and Angie sensed he had understood and valued the gift she was giving him.

A microphone came from out of nowhere as Angie and Owen reached the open door of the limousine. A fast-talking journalist moved in behind it. He was followed by a young man who had a videocamera perched on his shoulder. Angie caught a glimpse of the familiar television-station logo.

"Where's the honeymoon going to be, Sutherland?" the reporter demanded. "One of your own hotels? Or one of the Townsend resorts?"

Irritation flickered briefly in Owen's eyes, but Angie saw him suppress it almost at once. He gave the reporter a cool, fleeting smile. "The location of the honeymoon is a secret. I'm sure you can understand why. The last thing I want to do is find an inquiring journalist under the bed tonight."

The young man wielding the camera grinned, but another journalist was already moving in to corner Angie.

"Congratulations on your marriage, Mrs. Sutherland. This is going to be big news in the business world, as well as here in Tucson, isn't it? Everyone knows Sutherland Hotels and Townsend Resorts have been fierce rivals for years. And now a Sutherland has married a Townsend. I take it this means the rumors of a merger are valid? What about the possibility of a stock offering? Any chance the new Sutherland and Townsend might go public?"

Startled, Angie shook her head quickly. Microphones made her nervous. She was not accustomed to them the way Owen and the members of her own family were. She had always been shielded from the assaults of the business press. She did not like or understand the rough-and-tumble environment in which Owen and her relatives played expensive, dangerous games.

"You have it all wrong," she said to the reporter. "This is a wedding, not a business arrangement."

"A wedding that could spell a fortune for the two chains if it's true the two families have decided to bury the hatchet after all these years and join forces. Can we assume the merger will officially be announced today?"

"You mustn't assume anything of the kind," Angie said, frustrated by the man's persistence. "There is no merger. This marriage has nothing to do with business. Explain it to him, Owen."

Owen took charge before Angie could protest further. "I'm afraid you'll have to excuse us," he said smoothly as another reporter shoved a microphone forward. "We've got a plane to catch. You can talk to my new father-in-law and brother-in-law if you want more information."

"So Palmer and Harry Townsend are going to make the announcement?"

Angie held her veil out of her eyes and scowled at the man. "For the last time, there is no announcement to be made. This is a *wedding*."

"My wife is right. This is a wedding," Owen said as he guided Angie into the backseat of the limo. "And the groom is getting impatient. We have to be on our way."

He got in beside Angie. The driver closed the door very firmly and hurried around the big car to get behind the wheel.

As the vehicle drove off Angie turned to wave one last time at her mother, father and brother, who were still occupying the doorway of the country club. Her mother waved a hankie. Angie caught a glimpse of her father grinning broadly and saw Harry's bright red hair shining in the warm desert sunlight. Then both men were inundated by a sea of reporters and cameras.

"That was very sneaky of you to sic those journalists on Dad and Harry." Angie sat back in the seat and turned her head to smile at Owen.

"Better them than me. I've got more important things to do today." Owen's hand closed over Angie's. He lifted her fingers to his lips, and his eyes met hers as he brushed a kiss against the plain golden band she was wearing. His ring was a wide circle of carefully beaten gold, as utterly masculine as the man. Angie had designed and created it for him.

Owen looked ruefully at the plain ring he had given her. "I probably should have let you design your own."

Angie shook her head swiftly. She gazed at her ring thinking that even though she loved designing jewelry and had taken great pleasure in creating Owen's ring, nothing she could have designed for herself would have been as perfect as the gold band Owen had given her. The bold simplicity of the ring appealed to her. Moreover, Angie knew her wedding ring was not just a piece of jewelry; it was an ancient symbol, and she would treasure it as such.

"No. It wouldn't have been the same," she said fervently. "I love this ring because you chose it and you gave it to me."

Owen's mouth curved faintly, his satisfaction obvious. "And what about me, Mrs. Sutherland? Do you love me, too?"

"You know I do." Impulsively Angie leaned forward and kissed him full on his hard mouth.

"Umm." Owen's eyes gleamed as she lifted her mouth off of his. "Remember that, will you?"

"How could I forget?"

"You're right. I'm hardly likely to let you forget, am I? Not after everything I just went through."

Angie tipped her head slightly at the odd tone in his voice, but she could not think of a way to ask him what he meant. He would tell her that he'd meant what he said. He was a very private, very controlled man, and she'd promised herself she would respect that. He would change. Love would open him up soon enough, she knew.

"I suppose that reporter was right about one thing," Angie murmured as she gazed out the tinted windows at the lush green fairways of a golf course. "The business world will be speculating about Sutherland and Townsend for a while because of the wedding, won't it?"

Owen shrugged as he unknotted the elegant black tie that circled his throat. "It doesn't matter what the press says. Palmer and Harry don't mind, and neither do I."

Angie frowned. "It's just that it's annoying to think that some people might assume our marriage was for business reasons."

Owen slid her a quick glance as he reached for the champagne bottle chilling in a bucket on the console in front of them. "Your father warned me that you had a wide romantic streak in your nature. Better resign yourself to the fact that people are going to talk for a while. It's bound to happen. After all, everyone in the industry knows that the Sutherland and Townsend hotel chains have been rivals for years."

Angie gave him a wry smile. "Yes, I know. Ridiculous, isn't it?"

"The old rivalry? I wouldn't say that." Owen handed her a glass of champagne. "It's had its uses over the years. The public relations people on both sides got a lot of mileage out of the fact that each chain was always trying to outdo the other."

She turned her head quickly. "You're talking as if the famous hotel feud is now in the past."

"Maybe it is, in a way." Owen lifted his glass to her. "Maybe what we've got here is Romeo and Juliet with a happy ending. I've just married my rival's only daughter, haven't I?"

Angie bit her lip, thinking that over. "Yes, you have. But that's not going to change the way either chain does business, is it? I mean, not in the immediate future, at any rate."

"Would it matter?"

"No, of course not," Angie assured him in a soft rush. The hotel business was the last thing she wanted to talk about. She smiled again. "I've never been particularly interested in Townsend Resorts, anyway."

"I know." Owen's voice was dry. "Your parents and Harry made that very clear. They said you started drawing and designing things at the age of three and you've never stopped."

Angie glanced at her hands as they lay folded on the skirts of her gorgeous gown. "It's lucky my father has Harry to follow in his footsteps because I would never have been any good in the hotel business. I hope your family and friends won't expect me to become an expert."

Owen reached out to catch her chin between thumb and forefinger. He turned her head so she met his eyes.

His gaze was very cool and very firm. "No one is expecting you to start taking an interest in the hotel business. Hell, that's the last thing I want. Stick with your jewelry designing and the business of being my wife and leave the corporate stuff to me, okay?"

She nodded, relieved. "Okay."

"This is our wedding day," he added meaningfully. "The last thing I want to do is talk about Sutherland Hotels or Townsend Resorts."

Angie smiled tremulously. "I understand. I don't want to talk about the hotel business, either. Owen, I'm so happy."

"Good." He smiled, clearly satisfied. "So am I."

"So where *are* we going to spend our honeymoon?" Angie gave him an impish grin.

Owen's brow rose with easy arrogance. "A Sutherland hotel, of course. The new one on the California coast near San Luis Obispo. You didn't think I'd choose a Townsend resort, did you?"

Angie laughed and relaxed against his side. His strong arm went around her, holding her close. "No, of course not. The last thing a Sutherland would do is stay at a Townsend resort."

Owen kissed the curve of her shoulder that was exposed by the heart-shaped neckline of Angie's wedding gown. His mouth was warm and tantalizing against her bare skin. "But tonight a Townsend will sleep in a Sutherland bed, and when she wakes up tomorrow morning she will no longer be a Townsend."

Angie shivered and knew it must have been with desire. It was strange that such a fiery emotion could send such a cold chill through her.

Wedding day nerves, no doubt, she told herself.

THERE WAS ANOTHER limousine waiting at the airport when the Sutherland corporate jet touched down that evening. The sun had set in a blaze of fire off the rugged California coast. A velvet darkness descended as Angie and Owen were driven north to the magnificent new Sutherland hotel and spa.

The hotel crowned a jagged bluff that overlooked the sea. It was a wonderland of crystal blue pools, lush landscaping and exotic architecture. On the premises were a golf course, tennis courts and spa facilities, as well as several different restaurants, a nightclub and a poolside bar. Sutherland hotels were known for being worlds unto themselves.

"Well, well. Not bad. Not bad at all." Angie glanced around with an air of cautious approval as she stepped out of the limo. "Almost as nice as a Townsend resort, in fact."

"Bite your tongue, woman," Owen growled. "You're a Sutherland now, remember?"

"Funny, I don't feel like a Sutherland."

"You will by tomorrow morning. I'll make certain of it."

Angie blushed under the impact of the sensual promise in his gaze.

An hour later she stood on the terrace of the spectacular silver and white bridal suite and gazed over the night-shrouded Pacific. She had changed into the silver gown her mother had chosen for her. Not quite a nightgown and not quite an evening ensemble, the silk peignoir made Angie feel sultry and feminine. The only jewelry she wore—aside from her wedding ring—was a pair of sculptural silver earrings that almost reached her bare shoulders. Angie had designed them herself.

The luxurious honeymoon suite behind her was empty. Owen had vanished a few minutes earlier, saying he wanted to touch base with the hotel manager. He had told her they would be dining in the room when he returned.

Angie took a deep breath of the fragrant night air. This was the first time she had been alone since she'd awakened that morning, and it was something of a relief.

The Townsend clan was an exuberant bunch, always up for a celebration. Anything from a christening to a wake would suffice. But although they enjoyed a good party, it was no secret Townsends were very family oriented. One of the things her mother and father had liked about Owen Sutherland was that he did not have a reputation as a womanizer. Nor was he noted for being highly visible in the social world. He was rarely in the public eye and would expect his wife to stay out of it, also. That suited Angie just fine.

One small fact had bothered her during the past three months, however. She had yet to meet any of Owen's family.

It was another unfortunate example of bad timing and lack of opportunity, Angie reflected. The headquarters of Sutherland Hotels had been moved to Arizona a year ago, but Owen was the only Sutherland who had come South with it.

She did not know all that much about his past. He had lost his mother when he was very young, and his father had died in a plane crash two years ago. The rest of Owen's family, which apparently included an ailing stepmother, a sister who was traveling in Hawaii with her husband, a somewhat senile uncle and an aunt who was unable to travel because of a recent knee operation, all lived in California. Owen had told her that the family home was on an island in the middle of Jade Lake in the mountains north of San Francisco. He had also mentioned that his stepmother and his aunt and uncle spent a great deal of time there. Beyond that, Angie knew very little.

It was odd to be marrying a man whose family she had not met, Angie thought as she gazed into the darkness. Even odder that not a single Sutherland relative had been able to make it to the wedding of the head of the family. But Palmer Townsend had seemed unconcerned when she had broached the subject and had vetoed the notion of postponing the wedding until the families had gotten to know each other.

"Now, don't go worrying about the old feud, Angie," Palmer had assured her. "Owen Sutherland runs that clan just like he runs his hotel chain. They'll all do what he tells 'em to do. And he'll tell 'em to welcome you with open arms. Besides, what does it matter if they're a trifle upset about the idea of him marrying a Townsend? You'll be living down here in Arizona, not over in California. You won't have to deal with his family very much."

Owen had said something along the same lines when she had tactfully raised the issue with him.

"Don't worry about my family, Angie. You're marrying me, not them."

"It's not as if his mother and father were still alive and refusing to come to the wedding, dear," Angie's mother had pointed out. "These are just some rather distant relatives."

"One of them is his stepmother," Angie had reminded her.

"I don't think he's very close to her. Owen was raised almost entirely by his father, from what I understand. And you must remember that families are different. Sutherlands apparently aren't outgoing and emotional like us Townsends. Just look at Owen. Calm and cool as a stone."

Angie was still not entirely certain everyone was correct in his reasoning but she had been too much in love to argue. The wedding had been rushed through on the schedule Owen had requested.

And now, for better or worse, the deed was done. Angie glanced again at the ring on her finger. *For better or worse?* That seemed a bit morbid for a wedding night. Another of those strange little chills went down her spine.

The white phone on the clear glass table beside the bed rang, breaking the pall of moody uncertainty that had taken hold of Angie. Grateful for the interruption, she hurried through the open French doors to pick up the receiver.

"Hello?"

"Mrs. Owen Sutherland?" The voice had a dry, raspy sound, as if the speaker was deliberately trying to pitch it abnormally low.

"This is Angie. Angie Sutherland, I mean." Her new last name felt strange in her mouth.

"Congratulations, *Mrs. Sutherland.* I hope you're satisfied with the bargain you've made. I know your family certainly is."

"I beg your pardon?"

"Tell me, how does it feel to find out you've been used as a pawn in a business deal this big? I hope you had the sense to at least get a prenuptial agreement guaranteeing you your fair share. If not, you're going to be very sorry, *Mrs. Sutherland.*"

"Who is this? What on earth are you talking about?"

"So I was right. You really don't know about the plans your husband and your father have made, do you? How naive you are. I was told you were. They said you were an artistic type who never paid much attention to the realities of the business world. Easy game for Owen Sutherland."

"If you don't explain yourself immediately I am going to report this call to the police."

"He's going to divorce you as soon as the stock offering takes place, you know. The Romeo and Juliet marriage was strictly for publicity purposes, although the Townsends think it's for real. Townsends are so emotional, aren't they? Even when they're doing business. They fell for Sutherland's scheme hook, line and sinker."

"Please, you've got to tell me what this is all about."

"Why it's all about business, *Mrs. Sutherland.* Don't you understand? The whole thing is about business. It always is with Owen Sutherland."

"Stop it."

"Think about it. The wedding and news of the ending of the big feud will draw enormous attention to the stock when it goes public next month. Investors will love it." The raspy voice was almost conversational in tone now. "Your family all think they've pulled off a coup but they'll soon find out they've been duped. They thought they could deal with a Sutherland but they're way out of their league."

Angie told herself she should hang up. This was nothing less than an obscene call. But a trickle of a premonition was back. Something was horribly wrong. She could feel it.

"In two years or less the Townsends will find themselves powerless on the new board. Owen Sutherland will be running everything. After that it will be just a matter of time before the Townsends are eased out of the picture entirely."

"I don't understand what you're talking about."

"Of course you don't, you naive little fool. Why don't you try dealing with reality for a change? Ask yourself this question: Why should Sutherland keep you around after you've served your purpose? Oh, one more thing. Take a look outside the front door of your hotel room. I think you'll be very interested in what you find there."

Angie did not hesitate another instant. She dropped the phone into the cradle as if it were a snake. She should have hung up immediately, she told herself. Owen would be furious when she told him what had happened.

Why should Sutherland keep you around after you've served your purpose?

Angie found herself at the door of the hotel room before she was aware she had crossed the thick, white carpet. She turned the knob with cold fingers and opened the door.

An envelope lay on the floor outside the room. Angie picked it up and stared at it numbly. Inside the envelope was a fax of a press release from the corporate offices of Sutherland Hotels. A note in the right-hand corner advised that the release was to be held until the day following the wedding, then sent to all major stock analysts, business news dailies and a variety of other media.

> Sutherland Hotels and Townsend Resorts today announced a merger. The two premier hotel chains, long rivals for the high-end market, have joined forces in order to expand into the global arena. To raise capital, the new corporation, which will be known as Sutherland and Townsend, will go public with a stock offering next month.
>
> Anticipation of such a merger has been keen among industry insiders and stock analysts since the engagement of Owen Sutherland, president and chief executive officer of Sutherland Hotels, to Angela Townsend, the daughter of Palmer Townsend, was announced a few weeks ago. The merger agreement was signed on the day of the wedding.
>
> Owen Sutherland and Palmer Townsend were both quoted as saying the marriage heralded a new era in the growth of the hotel chains.

Angie stared at the press release until a noise at the end of the hall made her look up. A maid pushed a car around the corner and smiled quizzically when she saw Angie standing in the open doorway.

"Good evening, ma'am. Was there something you needed?"

Angie shook her head distractedly and started to step into the room. Then she thought of something. "Wait, please. Did you by any chance notice who left this in front of my door?"

The maid shook her head. "Sorry, ma'am. I didn't see anyone."

"Thank you." Angie closed the door and sagged against it, clutching the press release. She took a deep breath and tried to think.

It can't be true, she thought wildly. Then she remembered the reporters at the wedding and remembered how Owen had calmly suggested they talk to her father and brother.

Her father and brother. They must have plotted this with Owen weeks, perhaps even months ago. Mergers the size of this one did not get planned overnight or on a whim.

It was so like the other members of the Townsend family not to bother naive little Angie with pesky business details, she reminded herself bitterly. They had all approved of Owen and that was enough. As usual, they thought they knew what was best for Angie.

Angie leaped for the white phone and frantically punched out her parents' home number. There was no answer.

The hotel room door opened as she was slowly replacing the receiver. She whirled to face Owen.

"Angie? Is something wrong, honey?" Owen was wearing the beautifully tailored gray slacks and white shirt he had changed into earlier. He came quietly into the room and closed the door. He frowned at her in concern. "You look like you've seen a ghost."

"What I've seen is this," she whispered. She held out the press release with trembling fingers. "There appear to be a few minor details about this wedding someone forgot to mention to the bride."

2

OWEN RECOGNIZED the Sutherland corporate logo as he took the fax from Angie's hand. He knew instantly what he was looking at and decided quickly that somebody's head was going to be on the chopping block within the next twenty-four hours. It would most likely be the neck of his vice president in charge of public relations that would feel the ax, although it was hard to believe Calhoun had screwed up this badly. Calhoun, like everyone on Owen's staff, knew that when the president of the Sutherland Hotel Corporation said he wanted something kept under wraps, he meant it. People got fired for this kind of mistake.

It was possible, of course, that someone on the Townsend staff had been responsible for leaking the news a day early. The Townsends were a notoriously excitable bunch, not cool and controlled like the Sutherlands. Still, everyone had agreed the news of the merger should be kept secret until the day after the wedding.

Palmer had been as insistent on that point as Sutherland. He had said that Angie, with her romantic, artistic ways and her lack of a proper business perspective, might not understand why her wedding had been timed to coincide with the merger announcement.

No, the Townsends had no reason to leak the news, and there was no getting around the fact that the fax had been sent from Sutherland corporate headquarters in Tucson. This was a Sutherland error.

"Damn." Owen scanned the release. "This wasn't supposed to hit the streets until tomorrow."

"I'm not sure it has hit the streets," Angie said with an unnatural calm. "Perhaps it was meant for me."

Owen narrowed his eyes as he looked up from the release. It occurred to him that he had never heard that curious brittleness in Angie's voice before. Her words were almost always laced with some easily identified emotion: warmth or laughter, feminine curiosity or sweet, reckless passion—never this shaky coolness.

Owen studied his wife as she stood in front of him with her arms defensively crossed under her breasts. Slim and delicate, her fiery red hair pulled into a sleek knot at her nape, she looked at him with an injured, womanly pride.

Owen was fascinated, as he always was, with the startling turquoise of her faintly slanting eyes. Angie looked like one of her own jewelry designs, he had often told himself: elegant and feminine, with a quiet kind of strength and power.

The silk gown she was wearing clung to her gently curving breasts like liquid silver. Owen could see the outline of her nipples. He was suddenly, vividly aware of the rising heat in his own body. He had, after all, been anticipating his wedding night for three long months. Not nearly as long as he had been anticipating the merger of Sutherland and Townsend, of course, but long enough to play havoc with his fierce Sutherland self-control.

"Why do you say it was meant for you?" he asked, buying time while he tried to assess Angie's reaction. He was not certain what was going on in her mind. It was the first time he had found himself unable to tell what she was thinking.

"There was a phone call." She tilted her chin to indicate the phone on the bedside table. "Someone told me about the merger and then suggested I take a look outside the door."

Owen stilled as he assimilated that bit of information. Then a cold anger flared to life. "Someone called you to tell you about this?"

"Yes."

"What did he say?"

"I'm not sure it was a he. It could have been a woman. Whoever it was did not say much, only that I had been used as a pawn in one of your business maneuvers."

Owen waited. When Angie did not volunteer anything more he prodded carefully. "Was that all the caller had to say?"

"No."

"Don't you think you'd better tell me the rest?"

She shrugged. The silver silk flowed over her breasts with the movement. "There wasn't much more. Just that within a couple of years the Townsends would discover they were out in the cold and you would be running everything. Oh, yes, there was also the strong suggestion that when my usefulness was past, which would be immediately after the stock offering, you would divorce me."

"I'll destroy whoever made that call," Owen said. He crumpled the fax in one fist.

"Will you?"

"Count on it. I won't allow anyone to upset you like this and get away with it. Angie, you didn't take any of that nonsense about being a pawn seriously, did you?"

Hope instantly brightened her eyes. "Are you telling me it's all a lie? That there's no truth in the press release? Owen, I'm so relieved. You don't know how..."

Owen exhaled deeply as he walked across the room to the liquor cabinet and poured himself a glass of the French brandy he had ordered earlier. "The merger is a fact. Your father and I signed the papers this morning shortly before the ceremony."

The hope in her eyes died a quick death. "I see."

"No, I don't think you do." He turned to face her, drink in hand. "You're reading far too much into this."

"Am I?"

"Angie, you weren't told about the merger because the entire deal was meant to be kept strictly confidential until tomorrow. It was business. You're not involved in your family's business, and there was no reason to tell you what was going on."

"I don't think I believe that, Owen. I think I wasn't told about the merger because it would have made me wonder exactly why you were marrying me. Tell me, did my father make me part of the deal? Was that his way of trying to insure that my family didn't come out the loser in this arrangement? Or did he just see it as a fitting ending to an old feud? Townsends are all romantics at heart. He would have liked the Romeo-and-Juliet-with-a-happy-ending bit."

"The business side of this thing had nothing to do with the personal side."

"Do you swear that's true?"

"Come on, Angie, you know things don't work like that in this day and age." Owen smiled reassuringly. "This isn't a marriage of convenience or whatever they used to call them. I'm not a masochist. I'll admit I wanted the merger badly, but not badly enough to tie myself for life to a woman I didn't want."

"But you're not permanently tied to me, are you? You can get rid of me as soon as the stock offering is made. Whoever called me on the phone was right about one thing. The Romeo and Juliet gimmick is dynamite PR. Even I can figure that much out."

"Angie, calm down."

She ignored that, waving a hand wildly for dramatic emphasis. "I can see the headlines in the business press already. *Sutherland and Townsend end the feud with a wedding. New firm goes global.* People will love it, won't they?"

"Angie, listen to me," he said gently. "You've got it all wrong."

"Have I? Are you telling me that the timing of our marriage had nothing whatsoever to do with the timing of the merger? That it was all one incredible, amazing coincidence?"

Owen's jaw tightened. He wished he could cut this argument off with some smooth, simple explanation that would pacify Angie, but he knew that was impossible. The damage was done. "No, it wasn't a coincidence. But it wasn't nearly as Machiavellian as you're assuming it was, either."

"How can I believe that?" Angie challenged him with stormy eyes.

Owen felt his usually well-controlled temper start to rear. He made a deliberate grab for the reins of his calm, rational side, which had always served him so well in business. There was no reason it should not serve him equally well in his marriage, he told himself.

"I had been interested in doing the merger for over a year," Owen said. "I approached your father about it six months ago. He was receptive and we started talks. Then I met you and decided I wanted to marry you. The two events were entirely unrelated."

"Oh, is that so?"

"Yes. But when we realized there would be both a wedding and a merger, your family and I decided it made good business sense to combine them. The public relations opportunity was simply too good to ignore, what with the stock offering coming up soon."

Angie's chin came up angrily, her turquoise eyes sparkling with brilliant rage. "Why wasn't I told?"

Owen took a sip of brandy. "Because we knew you'd probably react exactly as you are now. You're a designer, an artist, not a businesswoman. Palmer and Harry agreed with me that you'd no doubt leap to a lot of wrong conclusions. Your mother thought we could tell you and that you'd understand if it was all properly explained, but she got outvoted."

"I don't believe this. It's as if you called a meeting of a board of directors and voted on my whole future."

Owen set his teeth. "Angie, we did it for your own—"

"*For my own good*. I know. Owen, I really detest it when people make decisions for me for my own good. Just when was I supposed to find out about the business side of this marriage?"

Owen sighed. "Tomorrow morning."

She stared at him. "Why wait until then? What difference was that supposed to make?"

"You'd have been my wife in every sense of the word by then," he reminded her quietly. "You would have known for certain that what I feel for you is totally separate and distinct from the business angle."

Her eyes widened. "You thought I'd be so overwhelmed with your magnificent lovemaking I wouldn't stop to put two and two together when I found out about the merger? That I'd be in some sort of sexual thrall to you by tomorrow morning? Good grief. I know you think I'm emotional and romantic, but I'm not stupid."

He shook his head, smiling slightly. "I never said you were stupid. I have nothing but respect for your intelligence." He glanced significantly at his ring. "And for your talent. But you are not business oriented, Angie. Even you admit that."

"Tell me something," she shot back. "Would you have courted me and asked me to marry you if you hadn't been interested in merging the two companies? Would you have gone ahead with the wedding if it hadn't been coupled with a good business opportunity?"

"Angie, you're not being logical," he said patiently. "I would never have met you if I hadn't decided I wanted the merger. Townsends and Sutherlands never socialized in my father's day. The feud was useful as a publicity gimmick, but it wasn't ever a mere PR creation. It was for real. It goes back thirty years and it would probably still be going on if my father hadn't died two years ago and left Sutherland Hotels to me. I decided it was time to end the feud and your father agreed with me."

"It was crazy," she whispered. "Years of craziness. I've always wondered what started it all."

"Something to do with the two companies attempting a merger thirty years ago. The deal fell through, and Sutherland lost some important financial backing, which Townsend later picked up. My father blamed yours. Your father thought it was all my father's fault that the deal went sour. After all these years no one knows for certain what went wrong, and as far as I'm concerned, it doesn't matter."

"Are you sure about that?" she demanded.

"Damn sure. Angie, I don't care what happened thirty years ago. I'm concerned about the future of my company, not the past. And I give your father credit for being willing to settle the feud. My father would never consider it. Lord knows we quarreled over it often enough."

Angie turned her back to him, giving Owen a view of her vulnerable nape and her glorious hair. His gaze skimmed hungrily down the graceful line of her spine. He watched the play of the silver silk gown over her sweetly curved buttocks and his fingers flexed tightly around the glass in his hand. *This is my wedding night,* he thought.

"Owen, I want to ask you something. Something important. Is the real reason no one from your side of the family came to our wedding that they all feel as strongly as your father did about the feud?"

"Old quarrels die hard," he admitted. "My family isn't like yours. Sutherlands aren't noted for being easygoing and open-minded."

"Did you think your people might like me once they got to know me? Were you counting on my charm and personality to win them over?"

"I'm not concerned with winning them over. I am only concerned that they treat you with the respect that is due my wife," Owen said softly. And if any of them did not, he vowed silently, he would cut off their income from Sutherland Hotels. He had the power to do it.

"On the other hand, why should they bother to get to know me when it's entirely possible I won't be a Sutherland after the stock offering is made?" Angie asked in a suspiciously bland tone.

Owen felt his temper start to slip again. He was not accustomed to the sensation and he did not like the feeling. He was always in control of himself, his business and everyone around him. Nobody manipulated Owen Sutherland.

His father had taught him to dominate any situation in which he found himself. This marriage would be no different. He would be in charge. The first step was to maintain his self-control.

"This has gone far enough," Owen said coolly. "For the last time, Angie, I didn't marry you because of the merger."

"Why did you marry me?" she asked. She did not turn to look at him. She was still hugging herself very tightly.

"Because I want you as my wife."

"Owen, do you love me? Really love me?" Angie asked in a small voice, still not turning. "You've never said the words, you know. I've been assuming so much. I've been telling myself that you have a hard time talking about your emotions, but maybe I've been making excuses for you because I was so desperately in love myself."

The brandy glass made a sound like the crack of a pistol shot when Owen slammed it on the liquor cabinet. He stalked across the room and caught Angie by the shoulders, whirling her to face him. He saw her beautiful eyes widen in surprise and trepidation.

"You don't need to make excuses for me," he bit out. "I married you. You are the only woman I have ever asked to marry me. You are everything I want and need in a wife, and I knew it the minute I saw you. We are in this together, you and I. We will make it work. You have my word of honor on it."

"If only I could be sure—"

He looked into her tumultuous gaze, gave a low, frustrated groan and pulled her into his arms. He covered her trembling mouth with his before she could finish the sentence.

Deliberately Owen set about using his own desire to ignite Angie's. He was positive he could do it. She had been responding to him beautifully during the past few weeks—sweet and hot, hovering on the brink of total surrender. Owen had gloried in the knowledge that he could make her react completely to him. He had used his sensual power gently, cautiously, not wanting to alarm her or take advantage of her. But he was getting desperate.

And she was his wife. He had a right to coax the response he knew she was longing to give him. If he could get her into bed, everything would be all right again, he was certain of it.

"*Owen*. Owen, please . . ."

He heard the feminine desire in her soft, pleading cry and felt her begin to lean into him. Her soft breasts were crushed against his chest. Her arms stole around his neck and her lips parted as he deepened the kiss.

Owen let his tongue probe the warmth of Angie's mouth as he slid his hands slowly up her spine. She sighed softly and her eyes closed. Owen felt her hips against his thighs, and his already aroused body tightened even more with a fierce, compelling need.

Owen was suddenly swamped with desire. He wanted to pull Angie onto the bed, strip off the silver silk and plunge himself into her. He inhaled the scent of her, part perfume and part feminine arousal, and he knew she was already becoming moist, welcoming, responsive. . . .

He could not wait any longer. She was clinging to him. Owen scooped Angie up in his arms and started toward the huge, white, canopied bed. He could only think of one thing, and that was his overpowering need to make Angie his wife in every way. This was his wedding night, and he was on fire for his bride.

In the morning she would understand that his need for her had nothing to do with the merger of Sutherland and Townsend. He would convince her here in their wedding bed. *With my body, I thee worship.*

"Owen..."

"Hush, sweetheart. We'll talk in the morning. It's all right. Trust me, Angie. Everything's going to be just fine. This is the way it's supposed to be between us."

He put her on the bed and leaned over to slide the tiny straps of the gown over her shoulders. Angie did not move as he slowly eased the fluid fabric to her waist to reveal her breasts. Owen sucked in his breath at the sight of her rosy nipples.

He gently caught one hard little berry between his fingers and squeezed carefully. Angie gasped, and Owen felt the shiver that went through her as if it had gone through himself.

Owen smiled and straightened. He watched her as he started to yank at the buttons of his shirt. Angie lay there looking at him with a growing wonder and a deep, questioning awareness that made him want to soothe and reassure her even as he ached to take her completely.

In another few minutes she would be his.

The knock on the door jolted Owen as violently as if he had touched a live electrical wire.

"Damn."

"Room service, sir," said the disembodied voice from the other side of the door.

Owen closed his eyes in brief, savage annoyance. Then he got a fresh grip on his self-control and managed a slight smile for Angie. "That'll be dinner. When I ordered it, I actually believed we might want to eat tonight. Obviously, I made a mistake. You stay right there, honey. I'll take care of it."

He went to the door and jerked it open, startling the waiter. The young man smiled nervously.

"Excuse me, sir—Mr. Sutherland. Uh, you ordered dinner, sir?" the waiter stammered.

"Right. I'll handle it. We won't need any help. We can serve ourselves." Owen summoned up his patience and reminded himself that he always had this effect on employees when he stayed in one of his own hotels. Tonight he probably looked even more forbidding than usual. He knew he was scowling.

"Yes, sir, Mr. Sutherland. And, uh, the chef sends his congratulations, sir." The waiter backed away, his face turning a bright red as he took in the state of Owen's clothes. "Sorry to interrupt. Let us know if you need anything else."

"I'll do that," Owen said dryly. He wheeled the cart into the room and closed the door.

He turned to look at Angie, who was sitting up on the edge of the bed, fumbling with her silver gown. She did not meet his eyes. "We don't have to eat this right now," he said suggestively. "It'll keep."

"*No!*" She leaped to her feet. "No, I'm . . . I'm very hungry. I hardly ate at the reception. And I couldn't eat breakfast. I haven't had much to eat all day, now that I think about it."

"Angie . . ."

"Here, I'll help you set that up." She darted forward and began yanking the silver lids off the serving trays. Fragrant aromas wafted up from artichokes and golden hollandaise sauce and perfectly broiled swordfish steaks. "Doesn't this look wonderful?"

Owen stifled an oath, aware that the moment had been lost. Angie had clearly gone from being on the point of sensual surrender to being a nervous wreck. His mouth quirked as he obligingly began dealing with the contents of the dinner cart.

"Shall we eat out on the terrace?" Owen asked politely.

"Yes. That sounds delightful." She carried the fish to the glass and white wrought-iron table on the terrace.

Owen followed more slowly, taking a long, deep breath of the night air to cool his clamoring senses. "Fog's coming in," he remarked casually.

"It is, isn't it? A bit chilly."

"We can eat inside, if you like."

"No, no, this is just fine," she said hastily. "It won't turn really cold for a while yet. And there's something very pleasant about the fog coming in off the ocean, isn't there?"

"If you like fog."

"Yes. Well, I do." She perched on the edge of one of the chairs and made a production of serving the food from the trays.

Owen sat down, watching her with indulgent amusement. "Why so nervous all of a sudden, Angie? I've kissed you before. I was always under the impression you enjoyed the experience. And this is our wedding night, after all."

"Please, Owen. Could we talk about something else?"

"Something other than our wedding night, you mean?"

"Yes, damn it."

He blinked lazily at the flash of temper and calmly reached for a crusty roll. "Whatever you like, honey."

The more agitated Angie got, the more Owen relaxed and told himself everything was going to be fine. She was such a fiery, hot-blooded creature, and that put her at a distinct disadvantage when dealing with someone coolheaded and self-controlled.

As long as she was nervous, Owen knew he would stay in command of the situation. It was only when she caught him off guard with that oddly brittle persona, as she had earlier, that he was at a loss.

They ate in silence for several minutes. Owen made no attempt to ease the situation. *Let her stew a bit,* he decided. When he eventually took her into his arms, she would no doubt collapse against him in total surrender, and that would be the end of the problem. The thing to remember when dealing with nervous, excitable creatures such as Angie was that they were their own worst enemies.

Owen was eating a slice of Brie from the cheese tray when Angie suddenly put down her knife, folded her hands in her lap and sat back in her chair.

"All right, Owen. I have done a great deal of thinking during dinner and I have made some decisions."

"Interesting."

"I would appreciate it if you could refrain from being sarcastic. This is a very serious matter."

"Making love for the first time? I agree with you. It is a serious matter, but I think we can handle it."

"Owen, please. This is not a farce."

"I know, darling. But you're on the verge of turning it into one, aren't you?"

She stood abruptly, liquid silver swirling around her slender frame. She went to stand at the terrace railing and gazed at the fog-shrouded ocean. "I have concluded that I cannot make a rational, intelligent decision about the future of our relationship tonight."

"You don't need to make any decisions about it," Owen said quietly, setting down his cheese knife. "The decision was made today when I put that ring on your finger in front of three hundred witnesses."

She shook her head quickly but did not turn around. Her hands were clenched around the railing. "I can't seem to think clearly tonight. Don't you understand? I'm confused and I'm frightened. I need time to consider everything."

"I see." Owen finally began to perceive where this jumbled conversation was heading. He tossed aside the monogrammed napkin and got to his feet. He crossed the terrace to stand directly behind Angie but he did not touch her. "Just how much time do you think you'll need to figure out that you really are married to me?"

"Until after the stock offering," she said in a soft, determined little voice.

Owen saw red. For one blistering instant he nearly lost his temper completely. It took him several seconds to regain his self-control, and even when he was sure he had himself in hand again, he still did not dare to touch her.

He forced himself to speak slowly and deliberately on the off chance that he had misunderstood. "What, exactly, are you trying to tell me, Angie?"

"That I don't want us to . . . to consummate our marriage until after Sutherland and Townsend goes public."

Owen could not believe what he was hearing. "The stock offering doesn't take place until the first of next month. That's three weeks from now."

"I know."

He put out a hand and closed it firmly around her shoulder. Very carefully, fully aware of his tightly leashed anger and his fierce desire, he turned her to face him. "You're saying you don't want to go to bed with me until after you find out if whoever called you tonight was telling the truth?"

She nodded mutely.

"How do you think that makes me feel, Angie?"

Tears welled in her beautiful eyes. "I'm sorry. But I'm scared, Owen. I've allowed you and my family to rush me into this marriage and now I'm wondering if I've made a terrible mistake. You know what they say about marrying in haste."

"You haven't made a mistake."

"Don't you see? You and my family should never have kept me in the dark about the merger. The telephone call and press release hit me like a ton of bricks tonight. They made me realize how willfully naive I've been about our whole relationship."

"Honey, that's not true."

"It is true. When you stop and think about it, you must realize I don't know you very well, Owen. I don't even know your family, let alone the true depth of your feelings for me. I need some time."

"Three weeks, to be precise, right? You want to see if I'm going to file for divorce after we take the company public. You want to see if this courtship and marriage have merely been a clever business ploy."

"That's part of it," she admitted in a choked voice. "But mostly I just want time to be sure of what I'm doing."

"Angie, don't forget the fact that your parents approved of this marriage. Your father and brother had no problem with the idea of doing the merger and the wedding at the same time. You know your family would never have gone for the idea of you marrying me if they hadn't believed you'd be happy."

"I know. What I don't know is how good you might have been at convincing them that you really care for me. Don't you understand?" Her voice rose in frustration. "That's the problem. There's just too much I don't know about you."

"Like what?" Owen demanded.

"I want to meet your family and find out the reasons none of them could be bothered to come to the wedding. I want to think about the fact that you kept the merger a secret from me. I feel I've been caught up in a whirlwind and now I want a chance to get my feet on the ground and make up my mind about our relationship."

"And you don't feel you'll be able to think clearly if you're sleeping with me?" he demanded, his fingers still clamped on her shoulder. "Is that it?"

"Yes, that's it."

"Damn it, Angie," he muttered, "you don't know what you're doing."

"I know. That's why I want time to think."

Owen shook his head ruefully. "That's not quite what I mean." He tugged her gently against him. Her body was stiff and unyielding, but he felt her tremble. He wondered what would happen if he kissed her. She was so responsive to his touch.... "My family is not going to be a good advertisement for me, honey. I see as little of them as possible myself."

"Owen, that sounds awful," she said into his shirt.

"I know. You say that because you Townsends are really into family. But that doesn't mean everyone else is."

"But don't you see? Sooner or later I'll have to deal with your family. I need to know what I'm getting into."

"Angie, I want you to trust me on this. Let me handle my family and the business. You just concentrate on being my wife and everything will work out fine."

"You're forgetting something, Owen," she said quietly. "That phone call tonight proves that you can't separate our relationship from the business of Sutherland and Townsend."

She had a point, and Owen knew it. He had kept the choice of which hotel he would be using for the honeymoon completely confidential, just as he and Palmer had kept the merger confidential. Yet someone had learned both secrets and had used them to drive a wedge between himself and Angie.

"And I seriously doubt that we can ignore your family, either," Angie continued. "No matter how much you want."

"We can give it a damn good try," he muttered.

She stirred restlessly against him and lifted her head. Her eyes were stark in the pale light that filtered from the hotel room. "And there's something else we have to resolve, Owen. Something I hadn't allowed myself to examine too closely until tonight."

"Damn. This list is getting a little tedious, isn't it? What else do you need time to think about besides my family and my business and my honorable intentions?"

She took a deep breath and looked at him, her face more sweetly serious than Owen had seen it. "I need to know if you really love me, Owen. That's actually the only thing on the list, when you get right down to it. Everything else I'm wondering about stems from that basic question. I don't know the answer."

His insides clenched. "Angie, I've told you, you're everything I want and need in a wife."

"Yes, but do you *love* me? That's what we need to find out. And then we need to see if you can admit it to me and to yourself. I need to discover if your feelings toward me are merely a result of your being physically attracted to me and feeling that I'm also an extremely useful business asset."

"Damn it, Angie..."

She straightened her shoulders. "I have decided we should delay our wedding night until we know for certain exactly what our relationship is based on and how long it's going to last."

Owen set his teeth. "I see. And just where the hell do you plan to spend tonight, Mrs. Sutherland?"

She blinked and gazed anxiously into the room behind him. "Well, this is a hotel. There should be plenty of rooms available."

Through an extraordinary act of will, Owen managed to quash his rage. But he brought his face very close to Angie's so that she would have no trouble seeing just how blazingly furious he was. "I'll be damned if I'll have my wife going down to the front desk of a Sutherland hotel on her wedding night to ask for a different room so that she won't be obliged to sleep with me."

Angie bit her lip. "I wouldn't want to humiliate you, of course."

"A very wise decision."

"I can see where it would be a bit embarrassing to have it get out that we didn't spend tonight together," she murmured apologetically.

"Embarrassing? I'd be the laughingstock of the entire hotel staff, not to mention the whole damn industry."

"Yes, we must maintain appearances, mustn't we?" she snapped. "After all, this is business. Everyone knows there are hundreds of thousands, maybe millions of dollars worth of Sutherland and Townsend stock about to go on the block. If you don't mind, I'll sleep out here on the lounger."

"You will sleep on the damned bed," Owen said through his teeth. "And so will I. We'll put a sword or something equally appropriate between us. Does that suit you, *Mrs. Sutherland?*"

Angie eyed him cautiously, obviously aware that she was on extremely thin ice. "Yes, thank you," she said very politely.

3

IN THE END, they used two king-size pillows Angie discovered in the closet rather than a sword. But as she lay wide awake on her side of the huge bed, counting down the minutes until dawn, Angie decided the pillows might as well have been made of steel. The barrier they created between her and her husband was certainly as sharp and formidable as any sword would have been.

She felt miserable. Guilty and hurt and angry and uncertain and just plain miserable. And the worst part was that Owen had apparently gone straight to sleep the moment his head had hit the pillow.

I'm doing the right thing, Angie repeated to herself over and over again as the hours crawled past with painful slowness. It became a mantra. *I'm doing the right thing.*

She realized she must have dozed off at some point because she came awake with a start shortly before dawn. She opened her eyes and found herself staring straight at a dull gray sea. For a few disoriented seconds she could not figure out where she was or why there was a huge white canopy overhead.

"You awake?" Owen asked from the other side of the bed.

Angie cringed at the coldness in his voice. *Well,* she asked herself, *what did you expect from your new hus-*

band after a wedding night like the one we've just had?

"Yes."

"Good. I've made some plans."

"Oh."

"Don't tell me you had any?" he drawled.

"No. Not exactly. I mean, I hadn't really thought about what we would do next. I know we're supposed to spend a couple of weeks here."

"That would be a bit awkward under the circumstances, don't you think?"

"I don't know about that," she said, thinking it through. "It's a lovely hotel and we're here now. We could spend the next two weeks getting to know each other."

"Angie, I am not about to waste the next two weeks playing the devoted bridegroom in front of a couple hundred people who happen to work for me and who will be watching us every time we leave this room," he stated flatly.

"I can see where that might be difficult," she retorted. "Playing the devoted bridegroom, that is. Especially if you're not. Devoted, I mean."

"Let's try this from a different angle," he muttered.

Angie turned to look at him, propping herself up on her elbow. Her first sight of him lying there, big and dark and dangerous against the snowy pillows, made her catch her breath.

Owen had undressed in the shadows last night, and she had carefully not looked at him as he'd climbed into bed beside her. Now she realized he was not wearing anything above the waist. She could not tell if he was wearing anything below the waist because the lower half of his lean, hard body was cloaked in a white satin sheet.

"Angie, are you listening to me?"

She realized she was staring at the broad expanse of his chest, thinking about what it would be like to twine her fingers in the crisp, curling dark hair there. She jerked her gaze up quickly, aware that she was turning pink. "Yes, of course."

He studied her, his crystal eyes narrowed behind his dark lashes. He had his hands laced behind his head and he looked very much at ease lying there in a strange bed with a woman who was not quite his wife. "All right, here's what we're going to do. I'm taking you to Jade Lake until after the stock offering."

"Jade Lake? I thought your step-mother lived there. And your aunt and uncle."

"They do. One big happy family. If we're real lucky my stepsister and her husband might drop in."

"If you don't like your family all that much why are we going to spend three weeks with them?"

"You said you wanted to get to know them, as I recall. I've got an office at the house. I don't use it very much because I don't go to Jade Lake often. But I should be able to get some work done from there during the next few weeks so the time won't be entirely wasted."

Angie sat up suddenly, pushing the strap of her silver nightgown hastily back up on her shoulder. She saw Owen's gaze rest on her breasts and realized her nipples must be thrusting at the silk. She hunched her shoulders to reduce the stress on the fabric.

"Now hold on just a minute," Angie said. "You're not going to dump me into a houseful of strangers for the next three weeks while you bury yourself in an office."

"This is the most logical way of dealing with the problem. It'll give you the chance to meet my family, and it will give you the time you said you needed to come to a decision. It will also keep our relationship offstage while we wait for the stock offering."

"I'm not so sure I like this. I think you've decided to stash me out of sight until after the new company goes public. You're afraid I'll jeopardize the interest in the stock, aren't you? People will start to question the strength of the merger if everyone starts talking about our shaky marriage, won't they?"

He shrugged against the pillows. "It's a strong possibility."

"Right. And if they question the merger, then they'll question the value of the stock. If they question the stock, you and Dad won't be able to get a good price for it when it goes public. And if the stock doesn't do well in the market, Sutherland and Townsend won't raise the capital it needs to expand."

"You've got it in one," Owen said roughly.

"I am not nearly as naive about corporate business matters as everyone likes to think," Angie declared with a touch of pride.

Owen inclined his head mockingly, but his eyes were grim. "The bottom line is that I sure as hell don't want you running around giving interviews for the next three weeks."

Angie was outraged. "I wouldn't give interviews."

"Reporters and competitors have a way of getting innocents like you to talk. If you were a starry-eyed bride who thought I was Prince Charming, that would be one thing. You'd just be shoring up the image of love conquering all every time you opened your mouth. But in your present mood I'm not taking any chances. I want you under lock and key until this whole deal is concluded."

"*Lock and key.*"

"A figure of speech. Let's just say I want us to have a lot of privacy in the next few weeks. The family home is on an island in the middle of the lake. No one can get to it without a boat and no one comes ashore without an invitation. Believe me, we won't be inviting anyone."

"You've got a hell of a lot of nerve to talk like that. If you think for one minute that I'm going to let you lock me up until you've launched the new company stock, you're out of your mind!"

"Angie . . ."

"You're right about one thing, however—you're no Prince Charming."

He moved so quickly Angie never even saw it coming. Owen clamped a hand around her wrist, hurled the pillows out of the way and dragged Angie across his chest. His eyes glinted.

"You owe me this much, Angie. I'm putting up with a hell of a lot from you. I think I'm beginning to figure out how the original feud might have gotten started. Apparently you Townsends have a nasty habit of trying to wriggle out of a bargain once you've made it. So far I've been deprived of a wife, a wedding night and a honeymoon."

"Now, Owen..."

"I'll be damned if you're going to screw up this stock offering on top of everything else. And if you've got doubts about behaving yourself for my sake, think about your own family. The Townsends have just as much at stake in this as I do. You're going to Jade Lake Island and you're going to stay there for the next three weeks. Understood?"

"My, God, you're cold-blooded, aren't you?"

"I'm trying to deal with a potentially disastrous situation here. This is called damage control. You're a walking time bomb for both the Sutherlands and the Townsends. And since you're legally a Sutherland, now, that makes you my problem."

"Thanks a lot." Hot, furious tears burned her eyes. "If I have to be kept out of sight, why don't you take me home to my own family, instead? I'm sure I'll be a lot happier there, and they'll be just as anxious to make certain I don't talk to the wrong people."

He slanted her a derisive glance. "Where's your sense of pride, Angie? Doesn't the idea of having your groom hand you over to your family the morning after the wedding night seem just a trifle embarrassing to you?"

He had a point. Angie had a sudden vision of trying to explain everything to the hotheaded, emotional members of her family. There was no telling how they would react, but one thing was for certain: the reaction would be loud and explosive.

Owen was right—she was not prepared to deal with Townsend dramatics yet. It would be humiliating to be returned to her family by a disgusted, cold-eyed husband the morning after the disastrous wedding night. She doubted that her father and brother would find her excuses satisfactory, and her mother would be in tears. They simply would not understand that this time, their so-called protection of her had backfired. Angie realized she needed time to figure out how to deal with her own clan as well as her problems with Owen.

She summoned up all her courage and tossed her hair over her shoulder in a defiant gesture. "I'll think about your suggestion to spend the next three weeks at your Jade Lake place."

"Yeah, you do that. Think about it real hard. On the way to Jade Lake." Owen sat up. "Start packing. We're leaving in an hour."

MUCH LATER THAT EVENING Angie decided she ought to have considered a third option to the problem of how to spend the next three weeks. She should have run away. Perhaps she could have hidden herself in one of the laundry carts at the hotel. Or taken a long walk on the beach and not returned.

The difficulty would have been managing to stay hidden. She knew Owen well enough to realize he would have tracked her down and dragged her back. *Anything to avoid embarrassing him and jeopardizing the merger,* she thought irritably.

The Sutherland family house crouched like a dark, predatory beast above a small cove on the eastern tip of a small, thickly forested island. Jade Lake was a large, deep body of water set in the mountains. The water was an unusual shade of jade green that darkened with the setting sun into a black, bottomless moat around the Sutherland fortress.

Fortress was the only word Angie could think of that suited the heavy, brooding old house. It had windows on all three levels, but no light seemed to enter through them. Everything inside the heavily paneled interior was dark, from the old Oriental carpets on the aging wooden floors to the heavy furniture in the rooms. The depressing avocado walls in the hallways made Angie long for a bucket of white paint and a large brush.

The moment Angie had stepped reluctantly through the front door shortly before sunset, she had known the next three weeks of her life were going to be extremely unpleasant.

On the other hand, as she sat down to the evening meal, she realized she could take cold comfort in the knowledge that Owen was not going to have a terrific time of it, either. He certainly did not seem to be enjoying the prospect of dinner in the bosom of his family any more than she was.

Angie toyed with her salad as she risked a speculative glance down the length of the polished dark oak table. The members of the Sutherland clan were a grim, depressing bunch—completely opposite in nature to her loud, cheerful, redheaded relatives.

"I must say, it was certainly a surprise having you show up on our doorstep this evening, Owen. Not that we aren't pleased to have an opportunity to meet your new bride, of course." Celia Sutherland gave Angie a wintry smile.

Owen's stepmother was a handsome, rather intimidating woman in her early fifties. She reigned at the far end of the dining table, a natural aristocrat with her patrician features and her beautifully tailored, tastefully restrained black dinner dress. Her hair, cut into a fashionable bob, was far too perfectly laced with silver to be natural in color; the artful shade was obviously maintained by an excellent stylist.

"Thanks, Celia." Owen gave his stepmother a laconic glance. "Knew you'd be delighted to meet Angie."

"I must admit we are all wondering why you're here, however," Celia continued coolly.

"We certainly are," Helen Fulton murmured from midway down the table. "Do we assume this has something to do with the merger?"

Owen's Aunt Helen was about the same age as Celia but she had allowed her hair to go elegantly white. Her pale gray eyes and high cheekbones testified to her Sutherland genes. The gray dress and pearls she wore gave her the look of a demure dove, but the icy glitter in her eyes indicated a more predatory sort of bird. That expression marked her as pure Sutherland, in Angie's estimation.

"You can assume whatever you want," Owen said. "Just so long as you bear in mind that this house is mine and I've got a right to bring my bride here."

"Hell, that's true enough, isn't it, Owen?" Derwin Fulton, Helen's husband, gave his nephew a grim look from beneath bushy white brows. "Your father left it to you along with everything else, including the business, didn't he? Wonder what he'd say if he knew you'd gone and married a Townsend."

White haired and broad-shouldered in spite of his years, Derwin appeared quite imposing in his dinner jacket. And he did not look the least bit senile, she thought in annoyance.

"I don't see that it matters much what Dad would have said," Owen replied with a bored, icy calm. "The only instructions he gave me were to take care of the business and make sure nobody in the family wound up on welfare. So far I've managed to do that."

Celia frowned. "Speaking of business, don't you think you owe us all an explanation, Owen? This news of the merger has been a great shock to everyone. You must have been plotting it for months."

"Mergers take planning. And that planning is best carried out in secret." Owen picked up his wineglass and took a sip. His eyes met Angie's in a warning glance.

"Well, I must say, your decision to rush ahead with the wedding to a Town...to *Miss Townsend,* here, was certainly unsettling enough," Helen murmured. "But to spring this other surprise on us is a bit much. We all know you run the company the same way my brother did, without regard for anyone else's opinion. But the least you could have done is consult us before carrying out something as drastic as a merger. With Townsend, no less. Derwin's right. Your father would have been appalled. And as for marrying a Townsend—"

"Don't worry, Sutherland Hotels is going to triple its net worth within the next few months," Owen interrupted coldly. "That should make the shock of the merger a little easier to take."

"Are you certain of that?" Celia demanded sharply. "Triple our net worth?"

"If the stock offering is as successful as Palmer Townsend and I think it will be, yes. The Townsends and the Sutherlands all stand to do very well out of this. Try to keep that in mind when you are being less than welcoming to my new bride."

Celia cast a quick, speculative glance at Angie. "Am I to understand, then, that this marriage is more in the nature of a business alliance?"

Helen looked up with acute interest. "That would certainly explain the matter, as well as your peculiar behavior lately, Owen. But if the marriage is just a business arrangement, why didn't you tell us at the start?"

"Yes, we might have gone to the wedding if we'd realized it was only a short-term arrangement for business reasons," Celia added briskly. "After all, it would have added a convincing touch to have had us there, don't you think?"

Angie sat frozen as the full impact of the women's words hit her. "I was told you were ill, Mrs. Sutherland, and that was the reason you were unable to attend." She looked at Owen's aunt. "I heard you were unable to travel because of recent knee surgery, Mrs. Fulton. Tell me, is Owen's sister Kimberly actually in Hawaii with her husband, or can I expect her to pop out of the woodwork any minute now?"

"She's in Hawaii, all right," Derwin said. "Bought the tickets right after Owen announced his intention to marry you. Tell me, what excuse did he make for me?"

Owen stepped in before Angie could respond. "I told her you had gone senile, Derwin. Actually, I had considered telling her the whole damn family was senile, but then it occurred to me that Angie and her folks might start to worry about the strength and durability of the Sutherland genes. I was afraid she'd back out of the marriage."

There was a collective gasp from the Sutherland clan.

Angie started to giggle. She could not help herself. The outrageousness of the remark appealed to her sense of humor as nothing else could have done in that moment.

Everyone at the table turned to stare at her.

The giggle escalated into a laugh. Angie blotted her eyes with her napkin. "Excuse me. But the picture of Owen sitting there at his desk trying to think up excuses for everyone . . . it's just too much. . . ."

Helen gave her a severe look. "Really, Miss Townsend."

Angie tried unsuccessfully to control her mirth behind her napkin, but it was useless. "Just wait until I tell Mom and Dad and Harry." She was aware of Owen watching her with wryly elevated brows, and her laughter increased until she thought she would fall off her chair.

Owen's dour relatives sat in stony silence. Derwin flushed a deep red and his eyes darkened in frosty annoyance. Aunt Helen looked pained, and Celia's disapproving frown tightened into a scowl.

"I'm afraid I fail to see the humor in this," Celia began coldly.

"That's one of the things you have to get used to when you're dealing with Townsends," Owen explained softly to his stepmother. "They frequently fail to react quite the way you expect them to react. And they find the strangest things extremely amusing. A very emotional bunch."

"Not like you Sutherlands," Angie recovered her composure enough to respond. "Your family appears to have a range of emotions that runs all the way from grim to depressing, Owen. I'll bet you guys have a really fun time when you get together at birthday parties and Christmas."

"Of all the nerve," Helen whispered ominously. "You have the manners of a street urchin, Miss Townsend."

Owen turned to his aunt with a cold, furious expression. Angie held her breath, afraid of the confrontation that was clearly about to erupt.

It was the housekeeper, Betty, a gray-haired, stoutly built woman in her early sixties, who saved the day. She came through the door at that moment and began clearing the table for the next course. She made quite a production of it, rattling dishes and causing a general commotion. When she reached for Angie's plate, she winked broadly. Angie hid a smile.

The moment of imminent confrontation passed. Owen subsided in his chair. He still looked ready for a fight, but it was clear he was not going to start the battle. Helen picked up her wineglass and took a deep swallow.

When a serving of poached fish was set in front of Angie, she discovered her appetite had suddenly increased dramatically. She picked up her fork with relish. The fish was excellent.

"About the merger and stock offering, Owen." Derwin spoke bluntly, having obviously made the decision to change the subject. "Don't you feel you should have consulted the rest of us before taking such a radical step?"

"No," said Owen. He took a bite of his fish.

"Well, I find that bloody damn arrogant," Derwin sputtered. "Your father would have discussed it with us, at least. Given us some indication of his intentions."

"No, he would have discussed it with me, but not with the rest of you. You know that as well as I do, Derwin. Now that Dad's gone, I make my own decisions. It's time Sutherland Hotels went after a piece of the international market, and the quickest, fastest, most efficient way to do that is to merge with Townsend. Now, if you don't mind, I'd like to discuss something besides business. I am on my honeymoon, after all."

"But if this marriage is just a temporary business alliance, why pretend to be on a honeymoon?" Helen asked with a pointed glance at Angie.

Owen looked at his aunt. "You seem to be laboring under a misconception here, Helen. This marriage is not a temporary affair. It's for real. Until death us do part and all the rest. You and everyone else had better get used to the idea."

Angie knew the warning was meant for her as well as the others. She wrinkled her nose in silent defiance and concentrated on her fish.

"If this was a genuine marriage and a genuine honeymoon, why on earth did you show up here today?" Celia demanded.

"For privacy. I figure it's the last place the reporters, insiders and analysts will be looking for me. They'll be busy staking out all the Sutherland and Townsend hotels."

"I wouldn't put it past 'em to find you here," Derwin warned him.

Owen smiled grimly at his assembled relatives. "I've given Jeffers orders not to allow anyone who is not family to dock a boat and come ashore without my personal authorization. Betty has been told to refer all phone calls to me."

"What on earth?" Helen looked stricken. "You're going to intercept our personal phone messages? You can't do that, Owen."

"Now see here, Owen, you can't just drop in here like this and start giving orders right and left to the staff," Celia informed him in frozen accents.

"Why not? I pay their salaries," Owen said. "And as I am also directly responsible for everyone else's income around here, I will give all the orders I want while I am in residence. This house is large. I'm sure we can all manage to move around in it for the next three weeks without tripping over each other too frequently."

Celia looked incensed. "Of all the high-handed, intolerable things to say. Your father always intended me to have this house. You know he did."

"Then he should have left it to you instead of me," Owen said easily.

Celia stared at her stepson in fulminating silence then apparently decided there was no point arguing. She swung her steely-eyed gaze toward Angie. "What about you, Miss Townsend? I take it you are going along with all this because of the money involved in the forthcoming stock offering?"

Angie looked down the long length of the table and smiled politely. "Were you speaking to me, Celia? In that case you made a mistake. My name is Mrs. Sutherland now. Mrs. Owen Sutherland. Not Miss Townsend."

There was another appalled silence. This time it was broken by Owen's shout of laughter. "Be warned, everyone," he said with a wide grin. "If you back a Townsend into a corner, she'll come out fighting."

It was one of the few times Angie had ever heard her husband laugh out loud. She turned to look at him in surprise, along with everyone else at the table. He got to his feet, still chuckling, and held out his hand to her.

"And on that note, I think we will say good-night, wife. Come with me, *Mrs. Sutherland*. We are, after all, still on our honeymoon. I believe it's time we went upstairs to bed."

Angie blushed under the gleaming possessiveness of his gaze. Then she folded her napkin the way her mother had taught her years ago, rose and put her hand in Owen's.

His fingers closed around hers in a crushing grip that spoke volumes about the fierce emotion coursing through him, but as usual his hard, arrogant face showed no trace of whatever he was truly feeling.

He led her out of the oppressive, dark-paneled dining room and started up the wide staircase toward the second level of the huge old house.

"That pretty much settles it," Owen said softly halfway up the stairs. "Looks like it's you and me against the rest of the family."

"Is it?"

"Afraid so. Sorry about that. I'm not well liked around here, as you may have gathered, even if I am one of the family." He reached the landing and led her down the hall to the suite of rooms they were sharing.

Angie considered his words. "You know, Owen, I don't see them as your family, precisely."

"No? What would you call them?"

"Your responsibilities, I think."

He glanced at her in surprise as he opened the door of their suite. Then he nodded slowly. "They're definitely that, all right. Dad told me from the time I was a small kid that someday I'd have to be responsible for everyone else in the Sutherland clan. He said it went with the territory. He left the whole damned bunch of them to me along with the business. Sometimes I wish I'd become an astronaut."

TWO HOURS LATER Owen lay in the massive four-poster bed that had belonged to his father and listened for small noises from the adjoining room. It had been quiet for some time in the small sitting room that formed part of the bedroom suite. Angie had been scratching around in there earlier but she had apparently settled down at last and gone to sleep on the cot.

Owen figured he would be awake for a long time, judging from the uncomfortable tightness in his loins. The thought irritated him. It was not right that a newly married man should be spending the second night of his honeymoon alone.

He had hoped the frustration factor would be minimal tonight since Angie was not sharing a bed with him, but he had been wrong. He had found himself aware of every movement she had made nearby, and his imagination had supplied plenty of vivid mental pictures to go along with the soft sounds of her undressing and getting ready for bed.

In fact, he realized ruefully, it was too damned easy to summon up an image of her high, gently curved breasts and elegantly shaped hips. He ached to see the sweet passion kindle in her beautiful eyes and watch her gorgeous red hair fan out on the white pillow. When he thought of all the times he could have taken her and had not, he wanted to kick himself.

The cautious policy had seemed wise at the time. He knew Angie had been as nervous around him as a doe in hunting season for at least two months. He had wooed her slowly, not wanting to rush her any more than necessary. He'd had to move fast enough as it was because of the merger announcement—which he and the Townsends had agreed should come at the same time as the wedding. But he had also taken things carefully with Angie because he had found himself feeling curiously protective of her. It was a new experience for him.

But his overriding concern had been to make Angie his own. Owen had been certain that once he had put a ring on her finger, everything else would fall into place.

He was learning just how mistaken he had been.

He'd taken one hell of a risk bringing her to Jade Lake after things had gone so wrong last night. He did not bother to run through the reasoning he had used on the others and on Angie. None of it was valid. He'd invented that nonsense about needing privacy. This house was far from private what with Celia, Derwin and Helen hanging around. When he'd married Angie, he'd had absolutely no intention of letting her spend a single night under the same roof as Celia and the others.

It was perfectly true the house would be useful for keeping the financial world at bay for the next three weeks. But Owen knew very well he could have found a way to insure privacy for himself and his unwilling bride without having to stay at the old family place.

That morning when he had awakened from his botched wedding night, however, Owen had made an uncharacteristically impulsive and reckless decision. He wanted to find a way to force Angie to confront the reality of their marriage. The fastest way to do that, he'd concluded, was to make her see herself as Mrs. Owen Sutherland.

Celia, Helen and Derwin had obliged him very nicely by attacking him as soon as he and Angie had walked in the front door. Owen had known they would, of course. It was inevitable, given his relationships with the members of his family.

It had definitely been a risk, but it had paid off.

Owen groaned and turned over on the wide bed. He stared out the window at the moonlight on the lake.

He had wanted to force Angie to start seeing herself as his wife and he had known that there was no faster way to accomplish that than to make her choose sides. Tonight she had passed the first test with flying colors. There had always been the possibility that she might choose her own side. Therein had lain the real risk. She could have declared herself a Townsend and thereby taken a stand against all of them, her husband included.

But she had not. Owen had tossed the dice and he had gotten lucky.

Were you speaking to me, Celia? In that case, you made a mistake. My name is Mrs. Sutherland now. Mrs. Owen Sutherland.

"Sooner or later," Owen muttered to the shadows, "You really will be Mrs. Owen Sutherland. We'll have our wedding night, Angie. And when we do I'll prove to you that you were never part of a business arrangement."

4

ANGIE CREPT PAST Owen's bed with all the silence of a ghost. Her bare feet made no sound on the carpet. The hem of her nightgown, another daring concoction of lace and satin from her trousseau, floated around her ankles. She was carrying a quilted robe and her slippers in one hand.

Moonlight streamed in through the windows. It revealed Owen's bare shoulders and smoothly muscled back as he lay sprawled facedown on the white sheets. Angie felt a sharp pang of longing and a deep, feminine curiosity as she studied her sleeping husband. He occupied the huge bed with a magnificent male arrogance that was not the least bit diminished by the fact that he was sound asleep.

She could have been in that bed with him, Angie told herself sadly as she tiptoed to the door. She had every right to be there. But she was afraid. That was the problem. She was *afraid.*

All the anguished questions that had sprung up on her wedding night haunted her more than ever now in the small, dark hours before dawn. She had to get some answers and she knew only one place to start. Harry might not appreciate being awakened at three in the morning, but that was his problem. In fact, he deserved it after what he had done to her. She was not going to forgive him readily for participating in the family conspiracy to marry her off to Owen Sutherland. Even if he had thought it was in her best interests.

Her brother could be as overbearing and paternalistic toward her as everyone else in the clan but Angie knew from past experience that he would level with her if she asked a point-blank question. And she intended to do exactly that tonight.

She let herself into the hall and closed the door gently behind her. Hurriedly she slipped into her coral-colored robe and slippers. Then she stood still for a moment, allowing her eyes to adjust to the darkness. There was a faint light glowing at the top of the stairs. Someone had obviously seen the wisdom of illuminating such a treacherous area at night. The soft glow would guide her.

Angie trailed silently along the hall then started cautiously down the stairs. She moved slowly, testing each carpeted tread for squeaks before putting her full weight on it.

At the foot of the stairs she paused again, orienting herself. She recalled seeing a phone in the kitchen and another in the study Owen said he occasionally used as an office. There were probably others but she did not want to traipse through the big house searching for them. Owen's study was closer than the kitchen. Angie turned toward it.

The door was closed but it opened easily when she tried the knob. Angie let herself into the dark room and went to the desk. The moonlight provided enough illumination for her to see a microcomputer on the desk. A telephone sat next to it.

Angie withdrew a tiny flashlight from the pocket of her robe. She held it in one hand while she picked up the receiver and began to punch out her brother's number.

She was still on the Tucson area code when a man's hand came out of the darkness behind Angie, cut the connection and calmly removed the phone from her fingers.

"Owen!"

"What's the matter, Angie?" He calmly replaced the receiver in its cradle. "Couldn't sleep?"

Angie struggled for composure. Adrenaline pumped through her, causing her to tremble violently. "Good grief, Owen. You scared the daylights out of me."

"Did I?" He leaned negligently against the desk, his arms folded. He studied her intently in the moonlight. He had put on a pair of jeans before following her downstairs, but he was wearing nothing else. He looked menacing—and thoroughly male.

"Yes, you did and you have absolutely no right to intimidate me like this."

"Who were you calling, Angie?"

"None of your business."

"Your brother?"

She glowered at him. "I said, it's none of your business. But, as it happens, you're right. I was going to call Harry. He owes me some answers."

"Why don't you try asking me the questions?" Owen suggested softly.

She lifted her chin. "Because I can't be certain I'll get truthful answers. Who knows what you'll tell me? *For my own good, of course.*"

Owen's face hardened. "Damn it, Angie, you make it sound like you're the victim of a conspiracy."

"That's precisely how I feel."

"Do you have to be so melodramatic about the whole thing?"

Angie took a deep breath. "I feel I can't trust anyone in this house. You've made it clear I'm virtually a prisoner here for the next three weeks. It's plain none of your family wants me here. And it's very obvious they all wish you had never married me. I do believe they actually have the nerve to think you married beneath yourself."

"Angie, honey—"

"I'm nervous and I'm angry and I just wanted to talk to someone from my own family. What's wrong with that? How would you feel if you were in my position?"

Owen groaned. He reached out to hold her. He eased her stiff, resisting body gently against his hard frame. "Angie, I'm sorry things turned out this way. I never wanted it to be like this."

"Then let me go," she mumbled into his bare chest. The warmth of his skin was oddly comforting.

"I can't. Where would you go?"

"Home."

"We already went over that." Owen stroked her spine with strong, soothing hands. "It would be embarrassing for you to go back to your family."

"I've decided I can live with the embarrassment. I'm more angry than embarrassed now, anyway," she muttered. "I'm going to strangle all of them."

Owen dropped a soft kiss into her hair, threading his fingers through her thick mane. "If you're going to try to strangle anyone, it should be me."

"Don't think the thought hasn't crossed my mind. Unfortunately, you're too big. Stop kissing my ear. I do not want any romantic gestures from you."

"Damn it, things wouldn't be like this between us if we had just had a normal wedding night."

"Sex wouldn't have solved the kind of problems we've got." She trembled and quickly moved her head as Owen deliberately lifted a swath of her hair and kissed her nape. "I said stop it, Owen. I meant it."

He reluctantly lifted his head and gazed broodingly at her. "You still want me, Angie, even though you're angry. I can feel it. You shiver when I touch you."

"That's a sign of nerves, not passion."

"Is that right? Well, I've got news for you, it seems like the same kind of trembling I felt when you were aching for me to make love to you."

Angie glared at him. "If you can't tell the difference between nerves and passion, that only proves how insensitive you are." She stepped out of his arms.

Owen sighed and ran his fingers through his hair in a gesture of pure frustration. "Three weeks, Angie. That's all I'm asking. Just stay here with me for the next three weeks until the stock goes public. Afterward you'll see I didn't marry you for business reasons."

"And then what, Owen?" Angie walked to the window and gazed forlornly into the night. "What kind of marriage can we possibly have after getting off to such a disastrous start? How can I ever trust you again?"

He caught hold of her shoulder. "Don't call me a liar."

She eyed him wonderingly, startled by the fierce pride in his words and the hawklike expression in his eyes. It occurred to her that there was real fury in him.

"All right," she said stiffly. "I won't call you a liar."

Owen released her shoulder with a muttered oath and turned his back to her. He shoved his hands into the rear pockets of his jeans. "I can't believe this. No one has ever questioned my word. *No one.* I do business with a handshake—my word is considered as binding as a contract. That's the way my father always operated and it's the way I operate. And now my own wife dares to imply I'm a liar and a cheat."

"I didn't say that exactly," Angie murmured. It was obvious she had seriously offended him.

"You sure as hell came close. If you were a man, I'd—" Owen shook his head in disgust. "Forget it. I've had enough of this stupid conversation." He swung around to confront her, his eyes still glittering. "If this marriage is going to start off on a battlefield, we're going to make some ground rules."

"You mean *you're* going to make some ground rules, don't you?"

He shrugged. "If that's the way it has to be, yes. Rule number one is that you can believe anything I tell you. I have never lied to you and I never will lie to you. Ever. Got that?"

Angie crossed her arms beneath her breasts and hugged herself as a strange chill went through her. She had never seen Owen in this mood. He was always so cool and calm and controlled.

"Well, all right," Angie said thoughtfully.

Owen's jaw tightened. "I suppose I'll have to be satisfied with that, won't I? My own wife will kindly deign to show a modicum of trust. Lucky me. Hell, I can't believe this."

"Obviously you had the wrong impression of me, Owen. I am not quite as naive or as gullible as you seem to believe. I am fully capable of thinking for myself and of evaluating the evidence I see."

"You think so?"

She smiled grimly. "I can reach my own conclusions. Provided I am given all the evidence to evaluate, of course."

"What's that supposed to mean?"

She drew herself up proudly. "It means, Owen, that as long as we are setting ground rules for this battle, I have a rule of my own."

"And that is?" He eyed her warily.

"And that is, that in the future, you will not deliberately withhold important information from me. I am not a child, and I will not allow you to treat me like one."

He scowled. "You are also not involved in the hotel business. I fail to see why I should inform you of every little decision I make that involves my business."

"I am not asking you to inform me of every little decision. Just those decisions that directly affect me."

"The plans for the merger and stock offering didn't affect you, but you're holding me responsible for not telling you about them," he shot back.

Angie nodded. "Definitely. Because as far as I am concerned they did affect me."

"Only to your way of thinking. How am I supposed to know which decisions you'll think affect you?"

Angie smiled. "Beats me. You'll have to be very careful and conscientious, won't you? Probably best to err on the liberal side, Owen. Just get in the habit of telling me everything and that way you won't go far wrong."

He stared at her in outrage. "Why, you little . . ." He broke off, shaking his head again. "I can't believe this. Who do you think you are?"

"Mrs. Owen Sutherland. For better or worse, apparently." Angie strode past him, feeling vastly more cheerful than she had a few minutes ago. She went through the study door.

"Angie, come back here. I'm talking to you." Owen stalked out of the study behind her. "Damn it, where are you going?"

"To get something to eat. I'm starving." She went down the hall toward the kitchen. "Dining *en famille* had a bad effect on my appetite earlier this evening. But arguing with you has sharpened it again. I hope your housekeeper is big on storing leftovers."

Owen did not say another word as he followed her down the long hall. When they reached the huge, immaculate kitchen he stood in the center of the tiled floor, hands on his hips, and watched in bemusement as Angie opened one of the two large white refrigerators.

Angie stood bathed in the glow of the refrigerator light and surveyed the shelves of neatly wrapped and packaged items. "We're in luck. Looks just like the deli section of a first-class supermarket." She bent to lift the lid of one plastic container. "Aha. Tuna." She tried another container. "Pasta salad. This gets better and better. Now all we need are a few crackers."

Angie chose two or three items from the refrigerator shelves and carried them to the table in the corner. She set down her haul and went across the room to flick the switch on the wall. The fluorescent lamps overhead winked and came on, illuminating the sparkling white kitchen. Angie started opening cupboards.

"You're going to eat all that?" Owen asked, his gaze on the cartons of food waiting on the table. He did not move from the center of the room.

"I told you, I'm hungry. Arguing always gives me a voracious appetite." Angie smiled with satisfaction as she spotted a box of crackers. "Here we go. All set."

She found a couple of knives and two forks in a drawer, then sat at the table. Owen still did not move as she arranged the goodies and started piling tuna onto crackers. When she had a plateful, she sat back and looked at Owen.

"Would you like some?" she asked politely.

Still wearing his bemused expression, Owen came slowly across the room and sat across from her at the small table. Without a word he picked up a cracker and took a large bite out of it. He chewed reflectively for a moment. When he was finished he popped the rest of the cracker into his mouth.

Angie helped herself to two crackers then eyed the pasta salad with interest.

"Angie?"

"What?" She scooped out a spoonful of the salad and put it on a plate.

"Would you mind telling me what is going on here? A few minutes ago you were mad as hell. Now you're eating like a horse and acting as if nothing happened."

Her eyes widened as she munched a forkful of salad. "Something happened, all right. We had a major fight. But now it's over and I'm hungry."

"Is this the way you always are after a fight?" Owen picked up another cracker.

"Usually."

"Even when you don't win?" Owen's eyes mocked her.

"Who says I lost?" she smiled sweetly. She was feeling sweeter, she realized. It was amazing what food could do for a bad mood.

"I've still got you locked away here in my gloomy castle, surrounded by a moat and several irritating relatives," Owen pointed out dryly.

"They are irritating, aren't they?"

"Very." Owen brushed that aside, his gaze intent. "Angie, why don't you feel you lost that argument we had in the study? Why aren't you still ranting and raving?"

"I never rant and rave."

"Don't fence with me. Tell me why you're suddenly in a much better mood than you were fifteen minutes ago."

Angie sighed and put down her fork. "I suppose because I realized something during our argument. Something important."

"What was that?" he pressed.

She met his eyes. "You have a great deal of pride, Owen. As much pride as any member of my own family. I understand that kind of pride. It makes me feel that maybe I wasn't entirely wrong about you, after all. You do have feelings about a few things besides business. It's kind of reassuring, if you want to know the truth."

He stared at her. "You find it reassuring that I lost my temper? If that's all it takes to make you feel more at home around here, believe me, I can accommodate you."

"I just said I appreciate your sense of pride, that's all. I understand it, and it makes me feel as though we might perhaps have something in common, after all. And now I do not wish to discuss this any further."

"Is that right?" Owen drawled, looking dangerous.

Angie picked up a cracker, heaped tuna on it and stuffed it into Owen's mouth. "Mother always said the easiest way to make a man shut up was to feed him."

ANGIE WOKE THE NEXT morning feeling surprisingly well rested. She lay quietly for a few minutes, listening for sounds from the adjoining bedroom. When she heard nothing she got up cautiously and peeked around the corner.

Owen's bed was empty. The covers on the bed had been carelessly thrown to one side. Owen evidently expected the housekeeper to perform the chore of making up his bed.

Either that or he expected his new wife to do it, Angie thought in annoyance. She stalked into the bathroom and turned on the shower. She certainly was not going to fall into the trap of waiting on Owen Sutherland hand and foot.

When she had finished showering, she pulled on a pair of jeans and a sunny yellow sweater. She saw the note stuck on the mirror over the dressing table when she went to brush her hair.

Angie:
I'd appreciate it if you would make up your cot before leaving the bedroom. Betty will be in later this morning to clean. I'd just as soon she didn't notice we're using two beds. Felt certain you'd understand.
Owen

Angie grimaced in exasperation, put down her brush and went into the sitting area she was using as a bedroom. She was not particularly surprised by the note. It was little wonder Owen did not want the housekeeper speculating on their sleeping arrangements. He had his male pride. It would no doubt be extremely humiliating for him if Betty noticed he was not sharing a bed with his new bride.

She had fully intended to make up the cot, anyway, Angie reminded herself as she tucked in the sheets and arranged the comforter. She was quite accustomed to making her own bed in her Tucson apartment.

The memory of the chic, Spanish-style apartment she had given up shortly before marrying Owen made Angie wistful for a moment. She went to the window and looked out. The sunlight had finally risen above the surrounding mountains and was sparkling on Jade Lake.

Angie considered the prospect of breakfast with Owen and his relatives and decided she would rather take a walk around the small island.

She hurried into the hall and nearly collided with Betty.

"Oh. Good morning, Betty." Angie smiled distractedly.

"'Morning." Betty eyed her sharply. "In a hurry?"

"Just going to take a walk," Angie explained.

Betty nodded grimly. "Don't blame you. This house can start to close in on a person. Been working here for over thirty years, so I'm used to it, but I expect it's a little hard on someone like yourself. Hear you come from Tucson. You're used to a lot of sun, I'll bet."

Angie examined the woman curiously. "This place is a little dark, isn't it?"

"In more ways than one. But there ain't anything wrong around here that couldn't be fixed up just fine if the right man and the right woman was to set their minds to it," Betty declared firmly. "All this house needs is some love."

"Love?"

"Yep. Houses need love just like their owners do. Owen Sutherland's gone a little short of a woman's love for too much of his life. Mother died when he was just a baby, you know. Father was all right in his way, but tough as nails, if you know what I mean. Raised his son to be just like him. Never give an inch. That's the motto of the Sutherland men."

"I see."

"Yep. Like I said, ain't nothing a good woman can't fix. You going to attend to that problem, Mrs. Sutherland?"

Angie was so startled by the personal question she did not know what to say. She blinked. "Uh... Betty, if you'll excuse me, I've got to be on my way."

Angie fled down the long staircase and out the front door. She spotted none of the Sutherlands as she made her way across the lawn, through the gardens and to the boat house. Jeffers, the combination gardener and handyman, waved and went back to work on an outboard motor.

Angie waved back then turned and started walking along the shoreline. The fresh morning air felt clean and exhilarating. As she strolled along the pebbly beach she got her first good look at her surroundings. Yesterday she had been too upset about the mess she was in to note much.

Today she could see a sprinkling of cottages and the small town of Jade on the shore of the lake. There were several boats scattered on the shimmering, smooth surface of the water. Early morning fishermen, no doubt. It all looked very picturesque, Angie decided as she heard footsteps approaching from behind. She knew without turning around that whoever it was, it was not Owen.

"I saw you walk down here," Helen said coldly as she came up behind Angie. "Thought I'd join you. I always take a morning walk, myself."

"Good morning, Mrs. Fulton," Angie said quietly.

"You may as well call me Helen. Owen will insist upon it. Owen's just like his father was. He usually gets his own way."

Angie shrugged. "Whatever you prefer."

"What I would prefer," Helen said, gaze sharpening, "is that this whole merger business had never occurred. But it appears we're all going to be obliged to go along with it. It's going to be a long three weeks, isn't it?"

"It certainly will be if we all work at it." Angie smiled grimly as she turned to face the older woman. "I'm sure that with a little effort we can all make each other perfectly miserable. You Sutherlands seem to have a talent for it."

Helen's eyes narrowed angrily. "You don't know what you're talking about. Take my word for it, whatever ability we Sutherlands have for causing unhappiness pales in comparison to the skill you Townsends have. I, for one, have not forgotten what happened thirty years ago."

"Really? What did happen?"

"That's none of your affair. It is family business, and I am not about to dredge it up at this late date merely to satisfy your curiosity. My brother wanted it buried forever, and I intend to respect his wishes. I just wish Owen had consulted the rest of us before he opened up this hornet's nest. I know this merger will cause nothing but trouble in the long run."

Angie studied her. "You seem very certain of that."

"I am. Townsends are nothing but trouble." Helen sighed. "We shall just have to hope that Owen knows what he is doing and trust that he's got the whole thing under control."

"He usually does, doesn't he?" Angie murmured.

Helen shook her head, her expression dark with foreboding. "He thinks he does, but the truth is, he's not enough like his father when it comes to running the business. Too many modern notions, that boy. My brother was always single-minded about Sutherland Hotels. Did things the old-fashioned way. Put the company first. And he would never have trusted a Townsend. Not after what happened thirty years ago."

"I don't know what happened thirty years ago, and you obviously are not going to tell me, Helen. But I can guarantee that when it comes to business, my family honors its contracts."

Helen jerked her gaze away from Angie's face and concentrated on the distant shore. "How long do you expect to remain Mrs. Owen Sutherland, Angie?"

The bald question shook Angie. Whatever doubts she was experiencing about her future, she certainly was not going to confide them to this bitter woman. She managed a polite smile. "The members of my family take wedding vows quite seriously, Helen. Just as seriously as they do their business contracts."

"Never mind the romantic nonsense. Just tell me how much," Helen said flatly.

Angie pushed a lock of hair out of her eyes and frowned. "How much what?"

"How much will it take to get you to leave after the stock offering? If you're reasonable, I'm sure we can come to terms. I should warn you, however, that if you're planning to clean up in a messy divorce, you had better reconsider. Owen is no fool. He'll make certain you get the bare minimum."

Angie sucked in her breath. "Are you offering to buy me off, Helen?"

"That's putting it crudely, but yes, that's exactly what I'm offering. You'll have your share of the new stock, I suppose. That should be enough, but it probably won't satisfy you. So I'm asking you how much cash you want to go quietly out of our lives."

"I've got news for you, Helen. Townsends never go quietly." Angie turned on her heel and walked into the woods.

OWEN STOOD at the breakfast room window, a cup of coffee in his hand, and watched broodingly as Angie turned her back on Helen.

"I suppose Helen tried to buy her off," Celia said calmly as she carried her coffee to the window and looked down. "Looks like the first offer was too low."

Owen's fingers locked violently around the handle of the cup but he kept his voice cool as he responded to his stepmother. "If Aunt Helen had any sense, she'd know that was the wrong approach to use with Angie."

Celia arched one brow. "Why would it be the wrong approach?"

"Angie's got her full share of the Townsend pride." Owen took a swallow of his coffee. "Believe me, it's the equal of the Sutherland pride any day. You think a Sutherland would allow himself or herself to be bought off?"

"Don't be ridiculous." Celia frowned as she watched Angie stride into the trees. "Your father always said there was no comparison between Sutherlands and Townsends when it came to matters of personal pride and integrity. He always said a Townsend would sell his soul if the price was right."

"Dad was never very rational on the subject of the Townsends."

"You think your judgment is better than his?"

Owen shrugged. "Dad never met Angie."

"Maybe not. But he certainly knew her father."

"He thinks he did. But I'm not so sure." Owen turned away from the window. "Palmer Townsend is as straightforward and honest as the day is long. I don't know exactly what happened thirty years ago, but I seriously doubt it was all Townsend's fault."

Celia gave him an odd look. "Be that as it may, we all know that Sutherlands have very little in common with Townsends. I still cannot believe you've actually married one, Owen."

"Why do you say that?" Owen poured himself another cup of coffee from the silver pot. He realized he was genuinely curious about Celia's answer.

"Well, for one thing, it's quite obvious this young woman is not your type."

"You don't think so?" Owen smiled. "What is my type, Celia?"

"Someone a little more refined. More sophisticated. Definitely someone with better manners than those that young woman displayed last night at the dinner table," Celia said tartly. "She was downright rude, and you know it."

Owen shrugged. "She had cause, as far as I'm concerned. No one was going out of his or her way to make her welcome last night."

"What did you expect? You ought to have known better than to bring her here. Why did you, anyway? I don't believe you just wanted privacy from the business world. You could have found that somewhere else."

"I had my reasons and I don't feel like discussing them. Let's just say that I expect my wife to be treated with the respect and courtesy due her from now on. Clear?"

Celia sipped her coffee. "I cannot guarantee how she will be treated. You know Uncle Derwin. He hates the very name Townsend. And your aunt isn't much better."

"What about you, Celia?" Owen asked softly. "How do you intend to treat her?"

"I feel very strongly that I have an obligation to honor your father's wishes in this sort of thing. You know as well as I do what he would have said if he'd known you intended to merge the companies and marry a Townsend. He would have preferred Sutherland Hotels to go bankrupt."

"I doubt it. Behave yourself, Celia. I'm giving you and the others fair warning. Anyone who hurts Angie will answer to me."

Celia slanted him a questioning glance. "You're very protective of her."

"She's my wife. I take care of what belongs to me."

"What a pity you aren't as concerned about the members of your own family. It seems to me charity should begin at home."

"Are we by any chance discussing my sister's new husband again?"

Celia's mouth tightened. "Yes, we are. You have no right to keep Glen out of the business, Owen. You know how much it hurts Kimberly. You have the power to give him a high-level position. Why won't you do it?"

"Langley's an engineer. He has zero background in the hotel business. I'll be damned if I'm going to put him into Sutherland at a high-level position, and we both know Kimberly won't be satisfied unless I do. Besides, what kind of man marries a woman and then expects her brother to hire him into the family firm?"

"Glen did not marry Kimberly in order to get a piece of Sutherland Hotels. He genuinely loves her."

"Is that so? Then let him go find a job and start supporting his wife in the style to which she has become accustomed. I'm not interested in financing that marriage." Owen slammed down his coffee cup. "Damn it, I should have known we couldn't avoid that particular subject. Thank God they're both in Hawaii."

"Kimberly and Glen are due back in California today," Celia said quietly. "They're planning to drive up here tomorrow."

"Great. That should certainly liven things up around here." Owen headed for the door. "Just wait until Angie meets my adoring little sister and her freeloading husband. She's really going to start wondering what kind of family she married into, isn't she?"

5

THE FOLLOWING MORNING Owen hung up the phone and sprawled in his chair, thoroughly frustrated. He gazed thoughtfully out the study window as he analyzed what he had just learned from the head of his public relations department.

Owen had been coldly furious with Calhoun when he made the call. He had fully expected to fire someone before the conversation was finished. But after talking to Calhoun, he had opted to wait for more information before making any decisions. The truth was, no one in the head office seemed to have been aware that the merger announcement had been leaked.

For the moment, at any rate, Owen was inclined to believe Calhoun.

The situation left a lot of unanswered questions, and Owen intended to get the answers. But, he told himself, the damage had been done and he had a more pressing problem on his hands. Namely a marriage that was a marriage in name only.

The knock on the study door was brisk and peremptory. Owen wondered which of his relatives had come to corner him.

"Come in." He did not bother to turn as the door snapped open.

"Either you take me across the lake to Jade or I shall steal a boat and make a run for it on my own," Angie announced dramatically.

Startled, Owen swung the chair around so he faced her. She was wearing snug-fitting jeans and a bright green pullover. Her fiery hair was drawn back at the nape of her neck and fastened with a gold clip. She looked regally defiant as she confronted him.

"Why do you want to go to Jade?" Owen asked cautiously.

"Because I shall go crazy if I do not get out of this prison for a while." She gave him a challenging smile. "Just think of how it would look in the financial press, Owen. 'Hotel tycoon locks bride away on remote island and drives her mad.'"

"I'm the one being driven mad." Owen stood up slowly. "For your information there's nothing to do over in Jade. There's nothing there but a couple of small shops, a grocery store, a café and a gas station."

"No offense, but that sounds a heck of a lot more interesting then what we have here. Are you coming with me or do I commandeer the boat from poor Jeffers?"

"I'll take you over to Jade if that's really what you want to do."

"It's not what I really want to do. What I really want to do is leave permanently and never come back. However as that does not appear to be much of an option for the next three weeks, I'll go to Jade for the day instead."

Owen looked at her and wondered how everything that had once felt so right could have gone so wrong.

"Damn it, Angie, I keep telling you it doesn't have to be like this."

"I'll be ready to leave in ten minutes," Angie told him, spinning away as he took a step toward her. "I have to pick up something in the kitchen."

"What's that?"

"A picnic lunch Betty is making for us."

Angie vanished down the hall, leaving Owen staring after her in amazement. He pondered matters for a few minutes then strolled out of the house and down to the dock.

He found Jeffers puttering with an outboard. The laconic handyman did not bother to look up from what he was doing with a small oilcan.

"Goin' over to town?" Jeffers asked.

"Yeah. Need anything?"

"Nope. Use the launch. It's runnin' real good. Your uncle's been fiddlin' with all the boat motors. Figured out some way of fixin' 'em up so they run cleaner. Use less gas. Seems to be workin'."

"Derwin's still tinkering?"

"You know him. Loves to fiddle with things. Always has."

"Yeah." Owen watched Jeffers work for a few minutes.

"Might be a good idea to take the little lady away from here for a few hours. Betty says things are kind of tense in the house."

"It's going to work out."

"Maybe. Then again, maybe not."

"Jeffers, you're a real ray of sunshine, you know that?"

"Bull. You got a lot of your father in you, boy. Going to be interestin' to see if the little lady can soften you up a bit."

Owen scowled. "I don't need softening up. I just need a little time to get everything back on track around here."

"If you say so." Jeffers hunkered down with the oil-can.

When Angie appeared a few minutes later with a wicker basket slung over one arm and a wide-brimmed straw hat on her head, Owen had the small launch ready.

He eyed the picnic basket as he helped Angie into the boat but he carefully refrained from commenting on it. He had a hunch that if he showed any sign of hope due to the fact that she had gone out of her way to arrange a picnic, Angie might just dump the contents of the basket overboard. He did not know quite what to expect from her.

Still, this business of arranging a picnic lunch was definitely a good sign, he told himself as he untied the launch. He was feeling much more cheerful now than he had been a short time earlier. Owen decided to reopen the topic of their marriage, but this time, he promised himself, he would be more subtle.

"You know, Angie," he said as the craft began to move. "I've been thinking."

"Careful. I'm not so sure thinking is one of your niftier talents. It's your clever thinking that got us into this present mess." She clung to her straw hat as the launch skimmed across the mirror-smooth lake. Her attention was focused on the little town perched on the opposite shore.

"Very funny." Owen sent her a glowering look. "The truth is, Angie, our present situation is not exactly normal."

"You can say that again." Angie pulled a pair of oversize sunglasses out of her purse. She put them on and peered at the shore. "What a lovely picture this would make. I wish I'd brought my camera."

"Angie, I'm serious." Owen wished he was not obliged to pitch his voice quite so loud, but doing so was necessary if he wanted to be heard over the roar of the engine. "Try to look at this objectively. We are married but we aren't. Not yet, at any rate. It's an unnatural state of affairs. It's causing a lot of unnecessary stress in our relationship."

"No kidding."

He glanced at her in annoyance and saw she was still concentrating on the upcoming shore. "Sarcasm isn't going to get us anywhere, honey."

"Nothing is going to get us anywhere until after the stock offering." She looked at him. "So I suggest we don't try to discuss it."

"You're being irrational and deliberately stubborn."

"I've got a right to be irrational and deliberately stubborn. I'm the offended party, remember?"

"What about me?" Owen retorted. "I'm a bridegroom with an unconsummated marriage. Talk about offended parties."

"You're just feeling grouchy because things didn't go quite the way you expected, that's all."

"I'm feeling damned annoyed because I haven't had a wedding night."

"Sex isn't everything, Owen," Angie said primly.

"It's sure as hell a start in the right direction when it comes to marriage."

"Time you got used to the fact that you can't always have your own way. Things are going to be a little different around here."

Owen took a firm grip on his resolve. He had to stay calm and rational if he was going to win this war. Logic told him that sooner or later Angie would be defeated by her own volatility. Self-control was the key here. He had it. She did not.

"Maybe you're right," Owen conceded as he eased the throttle back and let the launch glide into the small marina. "Maybe I am accustomed to getting my own way most of the time. I suppose it's a habit. I've been making decisions for Sutherland Hotels for so long that I guess I just naturally make them in the other areas of my life, too."

Angie slanted him a suspicious glance. "Well, if you can admit it, I suppose that's a step in the right direction."

"Thank you." Owen tried to sound humble and ingratiating. It was not easy and it definitely did not feel normal.

She smiled hesitantly. "It's not so surprising. Your arrogance, I mean. My father and brother have a major streak of it, too. Sometimes it drives Mom and me nuts."

"Maybe we all three feel protective toward the women we care about," Owen suggested gently as he coaxed the launch close to the dock.

"That's what Mom says. But I don't think that's it. I think men like you are just naturally arrogant."

So much for the subtle approach, Owen thought as he vaulted out of the launch and set about securing it to the dock. "Angie—"

"What happened between the Sutherlands and the Townsends all those years ago, Owen?" Angie scrambled out of the boat, clinging to her hat and the picnic basket.

"I told you, I don't know." Owen reached down to grasp her arm. "Dad would never talk about it very much."

"Do you think your aunt and uncle know the full story?"

Owen frowned. "Maybe. They've dropped a few dark hints over the years. But it's difficult to tell if they really know what occurred or if they're just being loyal to my father."

Angie removed her dark glasses and peered at him from under the brim of her huge hat. "Aren't you curious?"

Owen shrugged. "I asked your father straight out about it when we started the merger talks. He swore he doesn't know the whole story. All he knows is that the first merger fell through when the financial backers pulled out of the deal. He says the Townsends got the blame but no real explanations. As far as he's concerned, it's history, and that's exactly the way I feel about it."

Angie considered that. "I'm not so certain, Owen. It seems to me that your family is as upset today about whatever happened thirty years ago as everyone must have been at the time."

"I told you, my family is different than yours. Sutherlands know how to hold a grudge." Owen took the picnic basket from Angie and clamped a firm hand around her arm. He steered her along the bobbing dock toward the shore. "What have you got in here? It weighs a ton."

"A picnic's no fun unless there are a lot of goodies." Angie hesitated. "About your family, Owen."

"Forget my family."

"I can hardly do that," she snapped. "I'm surrounded by them, thanks to you."

Owen swore softly. "I meant, forget about whatever happened thirty years ago. It's not important any longer."

"Hmm. I'm not so sure about that."

He glanced at her and decided to change the topic. "Welcome to beautiful downtown Jade," he said, indicating the short street with its handful of small, worn-looking shops. "What would you like to do first? Watch them check dipsticks at the gas station? Or perhaps you'd like to tour the grocery store. I hear they recently installed a new freezer unit. Should be exciting."

"Let's just walk, okay?"

Owen shrugged. "Whatever you say."

"So long as I don't say I want to leave, right?" She gave him a challenging glance.

"Right," Owen growled. He paced beside her in silence for a while, mulling over tactics. Finally his curiosity prompted him to ask a question. "How much did Helen offer you to go quietly after the stock offering?"

Angie shot him a quick, searching look. "How did you know about that?"

"It was an obvious move. One of the three of them was sure to try it. I saw you and Helen together yesterday morning and figured she'd been elected to make the approach."

"I see. You're very cynical, aren't you?"

"I'm realistic."

Angie sighed. "No amount was mentioned. We never got that far."

Owen nodded. "She probably figures you're going to hold out for a big divorce settlement instead."

"She did warn me that I'd get a lot less out of you than I would if I took her offer. Said I wouldn't stand a chance against you if I tried to fight you in court."

"The issue will not arise. There's not going to be a divorce, Angie. We're going to work this thing out sooner or later."

She did not respond. Instead she strolled beside him in silence as they left the tiny village behind and moved among the trees that fringed the lake.

"I think this would be a good spot," Angie finally announced, coming to a halt.

Owen glanced around. They were standing on a bed of pine needles not far from the lake's edge. "A good spot for what?"

"The picnic, of course." Angie took the basket from him and set it on the ground.

Owen watched as she shook out a checkered cloth and spread it on the ground. Then she crouched beside the basket and began laying out an assortment of interesting sandwiches and snacks.

Owen settled down on the cloth. "I think I recognize that tuna."

"Nope. Fresh batch. Betty made it up special for us this morning." Angie handed him a sandwich and took one for herself. She lounged back on one elbow and studied the big house on the island in the middle of the lake. "Who built that fortress you call a home, Owen?"

Owen followed her glance. "My great-grandfather. Came out west to make his fortune. Did it with cattle. Then he went back east for a bride. Built that monstrosity of a house for her. It's been in the family ever since. One of these days I'll sell it to somebody who has some fantasy about turning it into a bed-and-breakfast place."

"You're not going to make it into a Sutherland Hotel?"

Owen grimaced. "Hell, no. It would cost a fortune to upgrade it to the level of the rest of our hotels. Not worth it."

Angie tilted her head. "You don't like that house very much, do you?"

"No. And it wasn't convenient for business, either. Dad and I never spent much time there. But after Dad married Celia, we came up here more often."

"Celia likes the house?"

Owen smiled wryly. "I think she sees it as the grand old family mansion or something. Celia's very big on old family stuff. Likes to play lady of the manor. Dad humored her, for the most part. That's why he never sold the place. But now that he's gone, I'm going to get rid of it."

"Have you told Celia and your aunt and uncle that you plan to sell the place?"

"Haven't really discussed it with them."

"They're not going to appreciate it."

"No," Owen admitted. "But they're not the ones paying the bills on that monstrosity, either."

"You can afford them."

He scowled. "That's not the point. The house can't be run in a cost-effective manner, so eventually I'll get rid of it. If I can. Lord knows, it's going to be tough to unload in this market."

"Do you view everything in terms of cost-effectiveness, Owen?"

He sensed a trap. "No, not everything."

"What about a wife? Would you expect your wife to be cost-effective? Hypothetically speaking?"

"That is not a hypothetical question." He put down his sandwich, reached out and caught her chin on the edge of his hand. She did not attempt to pull away. "I've got a wife. And she is definitely not cost-effective at all at the moment. But I'm not going to get rid of her."

Angie said nothing. Her eyes were very wide as she searched his face. Owen waited a moment before slowly lowering his head. He gave her every opportunity to avoid the kiss, but she did not even try.

"Angie..." Her name was a soft growl of swiftly mounting desire on his lips as he eased her onto her back.

He felt the initial resistance in her and then her arms stole softly around his neck. *She still wants me,* he told himself with hot satisfaction. No matter how much she challenged him, she still reacted with passion when he took her into his arms. Relief roared through him.

"Angie, honey, it's going to be all right," Owen muttered against her throat. He was aroused already, straining against the tight denim of his jeans.

"Owen, I shouldn't let you do this. I know I shouldn't."

"Relax, darling." He slid his hand down to her hip. "We're married, remember? This is the way it's supposed to be."

"Not yet. There's too much that has to be settled between us first. I have to know for certain—"

He slipped his hand beneath the green pullover and found one soft breast. Angie gasped, and whatever else she was going to say was lost forever. Owen slid one jeaned leg between her thighs. He was wildly impatient with her clothing now. Everything—buttons, snaps and zippers—seemed to be conspiring to get in his way. He finally realized that Angie was batting ineffectually at his hands.

"Owen, stop."

"Angie, relax. We both want this. It's natural for us to want it. We're married. Take it easy, honey." He soothed her with kisses that trailed down her throat to the V of her pullover. Underneath it, his thumb slid over a nipple, and Owen thought he would go out of his mind with the craving he felt.

"Owen, I said *stop.* There's someone watching," Angie hissed.

Her urgency finally got through to him. Owen lifted his head. "What the hell?"

The sound of an idling boat motor finally caught his attention. He glanced over his shoulder and saw the grinning teenagers in the speedboat cruising just offshore. He swore again—an earthy four-letter word that most adequately expressed his emotions at that particular moment.

The kids hooted with laughter and gunned the speedboat, racing off across the lake.

Owen scrambled to his feet hastily. "A married man should not have to go through this," he grumbled. "He should be able to make love to his wife in privacy."

"Just as well we were interrupted." Angie sat up quickly and began shoving items into the picnic basket. "I'm really not ready for that sort of thing yet, Owen. I've told you I want to wait. I would very much appreciate if you would stop trying to seduce me at every opportunity. It's not fair."

He glowered at her. "Not fair? I'm your husband, damn it. I'll seduce you whenever I please."

Angie shook her head firmly, closing the basket. "No, I'd rather you did not do that." She sighed. "I didn't think it was going to be a problem."

"Now what are you talking about?"

"I've been so annoyed with you since I found out about the merger and the stock offering that I thought I'd be able to handle the physical side of our relationship."

"You mean you thought you'd be able to resist me simply because you're mad at me, is that it?" Owen felt his spirits soar as he realized what she was admitting. He started to grin slowly.

"Something like that."

"But you can't resist me, can you, sweetheart? You want me just as badly as I want you, and when I take you in my arms the way I did a few minutes ago, you melt. Warm honey on a summer day. That's only right, Angie. I'm your husband. Why fight it?"

"I *can* resist you and I shall continue to do so," she announced imperiously as she got to her feet, "until I am satisfied with the other elements of this relationship."

"Stop calling it a relationship. We're married." But there was no real bite in his voice now.

Owen was aware that he was suddenly feeling much better than he had since his wedding night. He should have tried the physical approach last night, he told himself. Tonight he definitely would take a new tack with his recalcitrant bride. Sex, not subtlety, was the solution to his dilemma.

Angie glared at him. "You can wipe that stupid grin off your face, Owen Sutherland. I am not a complete pushover, you know. I would have stopped you even if those boys hadn't come along."

"Yes, dear."

"I am not going to let you use the—" she licked her lower lip "—the physical attraction between us to manipulate me."

"I wouldn't think of it." Owen reached down, picked up the cloth they'd been sitting on and started to fold it. He hoped the action hid the laughing triumph he knew was probably showing in his eyes.

"I mean it, Owen."

"I hear you, honey." He packed the cloth and hoisted the basket. "Ready to start back?" He gave her an innocent smile. "Or would you prefer to continue our hike?"

"I'm ready to go back to the dungeon," Angie muttered.

"Hey, look on the bright side. I'm not trying to get you to wear a chastity belt. Just the opposite."

ANGIE WAS QUIET on the return trip across the lake. She had started out this morning feeling very much in control of herself and the situation. Looking back on it, she realized that the midnight confrontation with Owen the night before last had given her a dangerous confidence.

She had sensed the passionate pride in her husband and had told herself it meant he had other strong passions, as well. She understood pride and passion. She could deal with those powerful emotions. Or so she had thought.

But now she had to face the fact that she was still as vulnerable to Owen's mesmerizing sensuality as she had ever been. She must be careful, she warned herself. She had to maintain her equilibrium in this volatile situation. She was very much afraid she would lose what little advantage she did have if she succumbed to her husband's lovemaking.

There was another boat tied up at the Sutherland dock when Owen eased the launch into the small cove. He frowned when he saw it.

"Visitors?" Angie asked eagerly. She would not mind having a friendly face around, she thought.

"More family." Owen got out of the boat and reached down to help Angie. "My stepsister and her husband. This should be amusing."

"I take it you're not on speaking terms with them?"

"Oh, we speak to each other. Kim and I used to get along fairly well. But things have been different since she married Glen Langley six months ago."

"Why? Don't you like Glen?"

Owen lifted one shoulder as he started up the path toward the big house. "The problem with Langley is that Kim and Celia seem to think he should be put straight into management at Sutherland Hotels just because he's married into the family. Apparently Langley feels the same way."

"And you don't?" Angie asked.

"Hell, no. The man's an engineer. He's never been involved in the hotel business."

"And you think he may have married Kim in order to get a chunk of Sutherland Hotels, is that it?"

Owen glanced at her. "I think there's a very good possibility that's exactly why he married her."

Angie smiled. "You don't think there's just the slightest possibility he might have fallen in love with her? Or is he too much like you in that respect?"

Owen came to a sudden halt and rounded on her, his eyes coldly furious. "What the hell is that supposed to mean?"

Startled at the sudden change in his mood, Angie took a step back. "I was just wondering if you're assuming your brother-in-law is not in love with Kim because you don't happen to believe in love."

"So help me, Angie—"

"Owen, you've practically admitted you're not in love with me. Yet you married me. What are we supposed to conclude? That you may have married me for business reasons, after all? In which case, how can you fault Glen Langley for marrying your sister?"

"You are really walking close to the edge, lady." Owen's expression was ominous. "I'd advise you to stop baiting me about what I supposedly feel or do not feel for you before you go too far. You said you didn't want to be manipulated with sex? Well, I damn sure don't want to be manipulated with words. Understood?"

"Oh, yes, Owen. I think we have an excellent understanding of each other. I guess it's true what they say about never really getting to know a man until after you're married to him." Angie swept past him to the front door.

She drew a deep breath when she realized she was out of Owen's reach. Mentally she wiped her brow in relief. She had pushed him a little too far that time.

"Well, well, well," an amused masculine voice drawled from the doorway. "You must be the latest addition to the clan. Nice to know I'm not the only one who had the nerve to marry a Sutherland. I'm Glen Langley."

Angie looked up quickly and smiled when she saw the good-looking, sandy-haired man on the top step. Glen Langley looked relaxed and athletic in casual slacks and a sweater. He had an open face with blue eyes that seemed to watch the world with a hint of sardonic humor. She liked him on sight. He reminded her of her brother, Harry.

"I'm Angie." She smiled. "I expect you've already been told who I am and why I'm here."

"Right. You're Owen's latest business acquisition, according to the relatives. But I don't pay much attention to them—a dull and depressing bunch."

"You noticed that, too?"

"The problem is they're all much too concerned about their precious hotel business. I'm trying to break Kimberly of the habit."

"Fascinating observation," Angie murmured as Owen came up beside her. "I've been having a few thoughts along those very lines, myself."

"Hello, Langley." Owen arched a brow. "How was Hawaii?"

"Sutherland." Glen acknowledged Owen with an affable inclination of his head. "Hawaii was fine until I found out why Kimberly was so hot to go on the spur of the moment. I didn't realize until we got there that you'd recently told everyone you were getting married. As you can see, we're home early. Sorry we missed the big event."

"Don't worry about it. No one else from my side of the family bothered to show up, either. Believe me, it wasn't a problem. No one was missed. Where's Kim?"

"Inside talking to her mother." Glen glanced over his shoulder into the dark hallway. "Here she comes. Kim, darling, meet your new sister-in-law. I've already made our apologies for having missed the wedding."

The attractive young woman who came to stand beside him had the grace to blush. Kimberly Langley was tall and sleek. She was wearing gray trousers and a cream-colored shirt that added to her look of patrician elegance. Her dark brown hair was cut in a heavy bob. She nodded brusquely at Angie.

"Hello. Mother and Aunt Helen have been telling me about you."

"Nothing good, I imagine," Angie said cheerfully.

Owen shot Angie a warning glance then looked at his stepsister. "For the record, Kim, I expect Angie to be treated with respect. She's my wife and anyone who doesn't treat her as my wife will answer to me."

"Nobody's arguing with you, big brother," Kimberly said smoothly. "We all understand that this is a difficult situation for everyone concerned. For the sake of the company, I think we can all manage to stay civil until the stock offering."

"Yeah, I had a hunch you'd see it that way. I'll be in my study if anyone wants me." Owen climbed the stairs, stepped around Kimberly and went into the house.

Kimberly followed him with her eyes, then turned to study Angie. "I hope you knew what you were getting into when you married my brother."

"As a matter of fact, I didn't," Angie admitted, smiling brightly. "But I'm certainly learning fast. Always nice to find oneself surrounded by a warm, welcoming family, isn't it?"

"Mother was right. You are rather rude, aren't you?" Kimberly swung around on one well-shoed heel and disappeared into the house.

Glen waited until his wife was out of sight, then his blue eyes met Angie's. The sardonic humor was gone and in its place was a more serious expression. "I apologize on behalf of my wife. I assure you, she only gets like this when she's in the bosom of her family. I've concluded that Sutherlands tend to bring out the worst in everybody. I always feel like an outsider when I come here."

"I understand." Angie went up the steps. "I've had the same feeling since I got here."

Glen chuckled as he followed her indoors. "I can't tell you how glad I am to make your acquaintance, Angie. Something tells me you and I are going to discover we have a great deal in common. I suggest we combine forces and stick together against these dark, brooding Sutherlands. What do you say?"

Angie smiled, grateful for a friendly face in the gloomy house. "It's a deal."

At that moment she felt the hair on her nape prickle. She glanced down the hall and saw Owen lounging in the doorway of his study, his thumb hooked in his belt. She knew he had overheard Glen's remark about joining forces against the Sutherlands.

Owen held her gaze for a moment, his eyes unreadable. Then without a word he went into the study and closed the door very softly.

6

HE SHOULD HAVE SEEN it coming, Owen told himself later. It was a natural alliance. The two outsiders in the family, Angie and Glen Langley, were bound to discover just how much they had in common.

Owen had watched the pair covertly during dinner. Now, as everyone made a polite show of having a cup of coffee together in the living room, he could see the battle lines shaping up rapidly. He wondered if he had made a major miscalculation. The possibility made him go cold inside.

When it came to business, he always knew just what he was doing. But when it came to dealing with family, he was not nearly so sure of himself.

Langley and Angie were sitting by themselves on a sofa near the window. They were having an animated conversation about Angie's jewelry design business. Langley appeared fascinated. In a very short while it would be Angie and Glen in a united stand against the whole Sutherland clan. If he was not careful, Owen realized, he was going to lose what little ground he had gained when he had brought Angie here. She was no longer going to see him as the lone wolf defending himself against the rest of the pack. He swore silently, remembering the feel of Angie's sweet breast filling his hand earlier that afternoon.

Owen wondered if this particular sort of frustration, the kind experienced by a bridegroom deprived of a wedding night, was fatal, or if the torture could go on indefinitely without actually killing the victim.

"Those two seem to have found something to talk about," Kimberly murmured as she sat beside Owen.

"Looks like it." Owen concentrated on the view of the night-darkened lake through the window. He thought once again of how little he liked this place. In the distance he could see the glimmer of lights in the cottages along the shore. The deep, endless darkness of the forests loomed behind them, and beyond the trees crouched the inky black mountains. The sight gave Owen a vague sense of claustrophobia. He realized just how much he had come to prefer the endless expanse of the desert to these deep-shadowed valleys and the vast lake.

"Owen, please tell me what is going on," Kimberly begged softly. "This whole thing is getting extremely confusing. At first Mother and Aunt Helen and Uncle Derwin said you'd gone crazy when you announced you planned to marry a Townsend. They said Dad would roll over in his grave if he knew. They said you'd betrayed his memory by getting involved with a Townsend."

"Nice to know everyone was so concerned about my selection of a wife."

"Owen, this is not some kind of joke. You're playing a very dangerous game with our futures, and as usual you're not consulting the rest of us. Now Celia and the others tell me the marriage is part of a business arrangement. They say you're merging the two companies and that the wedding was strictly for show. Is that true?"

"No. But I don't expect anyone to believe that." *Hell, even Angie doesn't believe it,* Owen thought glumly. *Not even Angie. The one person who really matters.*

Kimberly knitted her well-shaped brows in a delicate frown. "Owen, I know we haven't exactly been close in the few months since I married Glen, but you are my brother. Don't you think you owe me an explanation, even if you don't feel you owe the others one?"

"I've given everyone the only explanation they're going to get. It's not my fault no one's buying it."

Kimberly's eyes widened. "Don't tell me you've actually fallen for her? I don't believe it...I won't believe it. You've never let any woman have that kind of power over you. You're the original iceberg when it comes to love. You expect me to believe you got yourself seduced by a Townsend?"

"You could say that." Owen thought of how alive he had felt the first time he had met Angie, the sense of certainty he could not put into words—the need to have her that had pulsed through him like electricity.

He recalled how cautiously he had wooed her in the beginning, how carefully he had worked to coax her into marriage. How passionately she'd responded when he'd taken her into his arms, even when she was furious with him. There was no doubt about it. He had gotten himself seduced.

Strange. He had never thought of it in quite those terms. He had assumed from the beginning he had been in control. Now he wondered.

"Owen, be serious. We both know you're not the type to be swept away by a grand passion." Kimberly studied him intently. "You've never been in love in your life. I doubt if you even know the meaning of the word."

"I think we'd better change the subject, Kim."

"But I have a right to know what is going on."

"You know everything you need to know. I'm married. The Sutherland and Townsend chains have merged. There's going to be a stock offering in a little less than three weeks. What more do you want to know?"

Kimberly stirred her coffee, her eyes mutinous. "All right, be that way. If you won't tell me what you're up to, I certainly can't force you, can I? Lord knows you're in charge of the business. Dad made a point of leaving everything to you, just as I knew he would."

Owen turned his head to look at her. "What's that supposed to mean?"

"You know what it means," she replied bitterly.

"I make damn sure everyone gets his or her share, you know that."

"But ultimately you're the one in charge, just as Dad was when he was alive. You hold the reins and crack the whip. The rest of us are just along for the ride. You were always the son and heir. The firstborn. The one he cared about the most. The one he groomed to take over Sutherland Hotels."

"Be reasonable, Kim. You never had any interest in the business."

"I was never encouraged to have any interest in it," she retorted. "But that doesn't mean I don't care about it. Everyone in this family cares about it. Unfortunately we're all dependent on you. You run things single-handedly and you never ask any of us for our opinions."

"Who should I ask?" Owen demanded softly. "Uncle Derwin, who never showed an ounce of business sense and who has spent his whole life tinkering with gadgets? Or maybe Aunt Helen, who spends most of her life researching Sutherland genealogy and sitting on the boards of her favorite charities?"

"You're not being fair, Owen."

"Maybe I should ask Celia for her input, is that what you're suggesting? Come on, Kim. We both know your mother only cares about doing things Dad's way. If she doesn't think he would have done something a certain way, then she doesn't think I should, either."

"She's very loyal to Dad's memory, that's all," Kimberly said defensively.

"To the point of not being able to tolerate the idea that I'm now in charge. Look, Kim, the bottom line here is that no one in this family is qualified to run Sutherland Hotels except me. They all just want to be certain they're going to get what they think is their fair share. Dad was right not to leave everyone a chunk of the chain. I can see the board of directors' meetings now. We'd fight tooth and claw over every single decision, and nothing would get done."

"With this merger you'll be letting Townsends help make the decisions. How do you think Dad would have felt about that?"

Owen shrugged. "He'd have chewed nails. But he's not here, is he?"

Kimberly's mouth tightened. "Glen is here," she reminded him quietly.

"I've noticed." Owen slanted another brooding glance toward the pair on the sofa. Angie was discussing some element of jewelry design. As Owen watched she took off her ring and blithely handed it to Langley for inspection.

Owen wanted to get up, cross the room, snatch the ring from Langley's hand and shove it on Angie's finger. She had no business taking it off like that.

"Please, Owen."

Owen frowned as he realized he'd missed something his sister had said. "Please, what?"

"Please give Glen a chance. It's only fair. Give him a position in the company. Something important. Let him prove himself."

"We've already had this conversation. The answer is still the same. Langley can prove himself someplace else besides Sutherland Hotels."

"Damn you, Owen Sutherland." Kimberly got up abruptly, the coffee cup clattering on the saucer in her fingers. "Who appointed you king and emperor? You don't care about anyone else's feelings, do you? You just do what you want. You make all the decisions regardless of who gets hurt and the hell with everyone else."

"If Langley wanted to prove himself, he should have done it before he rushed you into marriage," Owen said roughly.

"You still think he married me because of Sutherland Hotels, don't you?"

Owen saw the suspicious brightness in his sister's eyes and felt a stab of remorse. He realized Celia was glaring furiously at him from across the room. He wished he'd never come to Jade Lake. *A mistake. The whole thing was a monumental mistake.* "I don't want to get into that argument again. Forget it, Kim."

"I'll try." She slid a meaningful glance toward the sofa where Angie sat talking to Glen. "After all, who are you to talk, big brother? It seems to me that if anyone around here got himself married because of Sutherland Hotels, it was you."

A raw fury roared through Owen. He clamped down on it with every ounce of self-control he possessed as he got to his feet. With an enormous effort of will he succeeded in keeping his voice very even. "I don't want to hear you say that again, do you understand? The one thing I know for certain is that Angie did not marry me because of Sutherland Hotels."

"Then why did she marry you?" Kimberly took a nervous step backward but she did not turn and flee. "Don't stand there and tell me she married you for love or for sex. You two aren't even sleeping together."

"Who the hell told you that?"

"Betty, of course." Kimberly took another step back and put down her coffee cup. "She says one of you is sleeping in the cot in the sitting room off your bedroom. She can tell because whoever it is makes it up very carefully each morning using a different method of folding the sheet corners than the one Betty uses."

"Maybe it's time good old Betty found herself another housekeeping job," Owen said through his teeth.

"Oh, come on, Owen. If you're going to blame anyone for the secret getting out, blame me. I asked Betty what was happening and she answered honestly, that's all. You may pay her salary, but you're hardly ever here. She's been loyal to the rest of us for years."

Kimberly turned on her heel and joined her mother on the other side of the room.

Owen watched her for a moment then headed for the terrace. He had never needed fresh air more in his life. He forced himself not to look at Angie and Glen Langley as he left the room.

"IT'S EATING HER UP, you know," Glen said quietly to Angie.

"What is?"

"The fact that she can't coax her brother into offering me a job with the chain. Kim felt badly rejected two years ago when she found out her father had left everything to her brother. Now her brother won't accept me and she sees that as another kind of rejection. Her mother and Helen and Derwin are encouraging the idea."

"Do you want a job with the hotel chain?" Angie asked curiously.

"Hell, no. I wouldn't work for Sutherland if he was the last guy on earth offering a pension plan and paid benefits." Glen grinned faintly. "But I'd give my right arm if he'd at least make the offer."

"For Kim's sake?"

"You've got it. It would mean a great deal to her if her brother would bend far enough to offer me a position with the company. In her eyes it would mean he was at least accepting her choice of husband." Glen shrugged. "Of course, that would leave me with a really big problem on my hands."

"Which is?"

"Not knowing what Kim would do if I turned Sutherland down. I've got a great offer up in Seattle. But I haven't told her about it yet because I'm not certain how she'll react."

"You're afraid she won't want to go with you to Seattle?" Angie asked gently.

"Yeah. That's about the size of it. Celia has really been pushing the idea that I should be working for the family firm. And she doesn't just want me to get any old job in the Sutherland chain. She wants Owen to make me a vice president or something equally impressive."

"She probably thinks that if her son-in-law had some status, she and the others would have some say in the business," Angie said thoughtfully. "Right now they're all totally dependent on Owen's goodwill and sense of responsibility, aren't they?"

Glen chuckled. "I see you've got this crazy family figured out already."

Angie frowned. "Not completely, but I'm working on it. I've got one really big question I'd like answered."

"What's that?"

"I'd like to know what happened thirty years ago to set off the original Sutherland-Townsend feud. No one seems to know all the facts."

Glen narrowed his eyes over the rim of his coffee cup. "More likely no one's talking. This crowd can be real secretive. Especially Helen and Derwin."

"I've noticed." Angie started to say more but she was interrupted by the arrival of Derwin, who had wandered over to the sofa.

"You two look as though you're enjoying yourselves," Derwin muttered darkly. His bushy brows were drawn together in a straight line. "Glad someone is."

"It is a bit grim around here, isn't it?" Angie observed dryly. "Do you folks always have this much fun after dinner?"

"You think you're very clever, don't you, young lady?" Derwin scowled at her. "But you're not half as smart as you think you are."

"I've suspected that, myself," Angie admitted. If she was all that bright, she would not be in this situation, she thought.

Derwin flushed a dull red. "Go ahead and laugh, but we know the truth. Won't pretend to know how you got Owen dancing on the end of your string. Always thought that, whatever else he was, he was too smart to be taken in by some fast-talking female, let alone a Townsend female. Guess I was wrong on that score."

Glen started to frown. "I think that's enough, Derwin."

"Not near enough," Derwin declared. "Miss Townsend here thinks she's fooling all of us, but she isn't. Want her to know it."

Angie set down her coffee cup with great care. "Just how am I supposedly fooling everyone, Derwin?"

Derwin's face grew redder. His eyes slid away from hers. "You aren't Owen's wife," he sputtered. "Not for real, at any rate. The housekeeper told Kimberly that you and my nephew don't even sleep together. Ha. Pretty odd behavior for newlyweds, if you ask me."

"No one asked you, Derwin," Glen said harshly. "I think you've said about enough, don't you?"

"Not by half," Derwin declared, gaining momentum. "She's a Townsend, and we all know Townsends can't be trusted as far as you can throw 'em. Like I said, I don't know how she pulled the wool over Owen's eyes, but she can be damn sure she hasn't pulled it over ours. She's up to some sneaky Townsend trick, by God. And she won't get away with it. Owen will come to his senses sooner or later."

Derwin turned and stalked off to join his wife. Helen's face was rigid with anxiety.

There was a short, uncomfortable pause before Glen spoke.

"Don't pay any attention to Derwin. He's been bitter for years because neither Owen's father nor Owen trusted him with an important role in the family business."

"Where is Derwin from?"

"Poor old Derwin came from a proper sort of background. He was the son of an established wine-making family in the Napa Valley. But he was never interested in the wine business. He likes to tinker."

"Tinker?"

"Sure, you know. Gadgets. He invents them. Even holds a couple of patents, although he's never made a lot of money on any of his inventions. Owen's father always considered him something of an eccentric mad scientist or something, from what Kim tells me. He and I have something in common, when you think about it."

"You mean the fact that neither of you can get a high-ranking position in the Sutherland family business?"

"Right. The difference is that Derwin would sell his soul for the privilege of being treated as an important member of the family. I'd sell mine just to be asked to take the job."

"It sounds like the real problem is that neither Owen nor his father ever bothered to find a tactful way of handling Uncle Derwin. The policy appears to have been to ignore him as much as possible. Which Derwin and no doubt Aunt Helen and the others all resented." Angie shook her head. "What a mess."

"Yeah, you can say that again." Glen lifted his cup in a mocking salute. "Welcome to the war zone, Angie. As you can see, we're all just one big, happy family around here."

For some reason it was the fact that everyone knew she and Owen were not sleeping together that bothered Angie most of all. It should not have mattered to her, she told herself. Surely it was Owen's pride that had taken the blow, not hers. She had not wanted to carry out this stupid charade of a real marriage in the first place.

Owen's pride. Angie had been raised with a dynamic brother and a powerful father. She knew that a man's pride was a formidable and extremely vulnerable thing. It was all tied up with his ego and his need to feel in control of his life and his world.

Her mother had ruefully explained to Angie that a man's pride was both a source of strength and his greatest weakness. A wise woman handled it with great care.

Angie glanced across the room and saw that Owen had gone onto the terrace. Someone—Kim, no doubt—

had probably told him the rest of the family was speculating on his sleeping arrangements.

Angie recalled the little note requesting her to make up the cot, which had been stuck on the dressing table mirror that first morning. She had obliged, but now the truth was out, thanks to Betty.

Owen's pride would be so much bloody meat at the moment.

Angie smiled wryly at Glen and got to her feet. "Will you excuse me?"

"Sure." Glen gave her an odd look. "I don't pretend to know what's going on between you and Sutherland, but my advice is not to let the rest of the family get to you."

"The only one who gets to me is Owen," Angie told him softly.

"I know how you feel. The only one who gets to me is Kim."

Angie nodded in understanding and moved toward the French doors that opened onto the terrace. She could feel the eyes of the Sutherland family on her as she stepped into the cool darkness.

She did not see Owen at first. Angie went slowly toward the low stone wall that surrounded the terrace, wondering if Owen had taken a walk. She decided to leave the terrace and see if he had taken the path to the boat house.

"Hello, Angie. Thinking of making a run for the boat?"

"Owen! Good grief, I didn't even see you."

"Obviously." He was standing so still in the shadows of a tree she would have walked right past him if he had not spoken.

"Did you come out for some fresh air?" she asked hesitantly.

"You could say that. Why did you come out? It looked to me like you were having a great time talking to Langley."

"I like Glen," Angie said softly. She took a couple of steps closer to him, trying to gauge his mood. Her eyes were adjusting to the shadows, and she could see that Owen had one shoulder propped against the tree trunk. His arms were folded across his chest in that subtly arrogant manner he had.

"I know you like Langley. How could you not like him? After all, you two have so much in common," Owen said. "Just you and him against the rest of us, isn't it?"

Angie shivered at the dangerous softness in his voice. She realized how coldly angry Owen was. A startling notion occurred to her. "Are you jealous, Owen?"

"Hell, no. I've never let a woman make me jealous in my life. But I can recognize an explosive situation when I see one and that's just what I see shaping up here. You get any more friendly with my sister's husband and we're all going to have a big problem on our hands."

"There is nothing between Glen and me. He loves your sister very much. As far as I can figure out, that's the only reason he's willing to put up with you and the rest of the family," Angie said.

"So he's started crying on your shoulder already, is that it? Didn't take long. But, then, maybe you cried on his shoulder first, hmm? Did you tell him you haven't slept with your new husband yet?"

Angie felt her temper start to flare. "I never said a word about our sleeping arrangements."

"Is that a fact? Everyone sure as hell seems to know about them."

"That's not my fault. As a favor to you, I've made up that stupid cot in the sitting room every single morning since we got here."

"Yeah? Well, you didn't do a very good job of it, did you? Apparently Betty noticed right off that someone was sleeping in the sitting room."

"If you don't like the way I make the bed, you can do it," Angie retorted.

"If you were sleeping with me like you should be, nobody would have noticed a damn thing. There wouldn't have been anything to notice. Now the whole blasted family knows I've got a wife who won't even share my bed."

Angie took a deep, steadying breath. She sensed that the argument was threatening to roar out of control, and she was not certain what to expect if it did. "I'm sorry, Owen. I tried to make it look as though we were both using the main bed."

"I should never have brought you here."

"No. On that we agree." Angie looked at him. "We can always leave."

He gave her a disbelieving look. "Are you out of your mind? I'm not walking out of here now. I'll be damned if I'll let them force me out of my own home."

"Owen, you don't even like this place."

"That's not the point. The point is I won't let that bunch drive me off. And I won't let them think I've fallen victim to some Townsend con job."

Angie lost her fragile grip on her temper. "As it happens, we have something in common there, Owen Sutherland. I do not appreciate the fact that your entire family seems to feel I've pulled a fast one. Your Uncle Derwin believes you've been duped by Townsends. He says I've got you dancing on the end of my string. He implied I seduced you or something."

"Why don't you try it?"

"Try what?" Angie was completely exasperated.

"Seducing me. You're my wife, aren't you? You were supposed to be on my side in this war, Angie. I thought you'd figured that out. You said you understood about pride. It seems to me that if you really cared about my pride, you'd do your duty as a wife."

"I do understand your pride. But I've got some pride of my own," she shot back. "And a wife isn't supposed to sleep with her husband out of a sense of duty. She's supposed to sleep with him because she loves him."

"So where's the problem? You love me, Angie. You said so yourself on our wedding day."

"That was three whole days ago," she raged.

Owen smiled dangerously, showing his teeth. "No kidding. Three whole days and already you've fallen out of love with me. And here I thought your love would last a lifetime. I guess everyone in there was right, after all."

"What are you talking about?"

"I was duped by a Townsend. Had the wool pulled over my eyes in a major way. Yes, ma'am, you've made a real fool out of me, haven't you? I'm the laughingstock of my own family."

Angie was so furious she resorted to stamping one foot. "Damn you, Owen Sutherland. You're twisting this all up and you're doing it deliberately."

"You're the one who's twisted everything up, Angie. If you'd behaved like a wife is supposed to behave, we wouldn't be in this idiotic situation."

"Don't you tell me how a wife is supposed to behave. You know nothing about how a marriage is supposed to work. I have never met anyone less qualified to lecture on the subject of a proper marriage."

"Don't worry, I'm learning how this marriage works real fast. My wife sleeps in her own bed and gets real chummy with my sister's husband at the first opportunity. Should be interesting to see what happens next."

"Don't you dare drag Glen into this. He's got nothing to do with any of it." Angie was seething.

"I didn't drag Langley into this. You did."

"It's your own fault you don't get along with him, you know."

"Is that a fact?"

"Yes, it is," Angie informed him stoutly. "And I'll tell you something else. It's your own fault you've got troubles dealing with your sister. You want some advice, Mr. Sutherland?"

"From a wife who's a wife in name only? Not particularly."

"Well, you're going to get it, whether you want it or not," Angie told him through clenched teeth. "I can tell you how to solve a lot of your family problems in one blow."

"Oh, yeah? How?"

"Offer Glen a decent position in your company."

*"What?"*Owen stared at her, his eyes glittering with astonished fury. For a moment he did not move. "That does it," he finally bit out in a savage voice. "That really tears it, lady. I've been damned patient with you, but this time you've gone too far. You are not going to start telling me how to run my company."

"Owen, *no*." Angie hastily stepped back again, but it was too late.

Owen came away from the tree trunk in a swift, fluid motion that gave Angie no chance to escape. Before she realized what he intended, he had bent low, caught her around the waist and slung her over his shoulder like a bag of laundry.

"Owen, put me down this instant." Angie pounded on his broad back as he started up the terrace steps.

"The next time I put you down, lady, it will be in my bed."

He strode across the terrace, the heels of his boots ringing on the stones. He carried Angie through the open French doors and into the living room where the rest of the family fell into shocked silence.

"Good night, everyone," Owen said calmly as he walked through the room. "I realize it's early yet, but Angie says she wants to go to bed. I've decided to join her. You know how it is with newlyweds."

Angie groaned, torn between an insane desire to laugh and an equally strong wish to yell like a shrew. This was certainly a side of Owen she had never before witnessed, she thought ruefully.

A man's pride was, indeed, a dangerous thing to attack. She should have known the risk she was taking when she confronted Owen on the terrace. She had done nothing less than wave a red flag at an already seriously annoyed bull.

7

OWEN CARRIED ANGIE down the second-floor hall and into the master bedroom where he dumped her unceremoniously onto the big, four-poster bed. He braced one hand on a heavily carved post and stood glowering at her with a gleaming challenge in his eyes.

"Well?" he demanded.

"Well, what?" Angie sat up, brushing hair out of her eyes. She curled her legs beneath her and primly straightened her calf-length skirt so that it covered her knees.

"Aren't you going to start screaming or something? Don't you want Langley to rush to the rescue?"

"Not particularly." Angie fussed with the clip in her hair, which had come undone. Her fingers were trembling so badly she could not manage to close it. She tossed the clip onto the bedside table, hoping the seemingly casual action would conceal her nervousness.

Owen deliberately put one knee on the bed. The thick mattress gave beneath his weight. "Why don't you want Langley to come running?"

"I don't need rescuing from my own husband." Angie smiled tentatively, knowing where this scene was going.

The die had been cast in the heat of the moment downstairs. She accepted that the time had come to stop rejecting Owen on the physical level. She was beginning to understand that this was the only way in which he knew how to communicate with her. She had been depriving him of this source of intimacy because it required such an emotional risk on her part. But maybe it was time to take that risk. He was her husband and he wanted her.

She had to be brave tonight, Angie decided. Her intuition told her things had reached a flashpoint in her relationship with Owen.

"So you don't need rescuing from your husband?" Owen's hand closed around her leg, warm and strong and relentless. "If you're talking about me, I should warn you I don't feel much like a husband yet, Angie."

"Do you feel single?"

"No." He shook his head slowly and deliberately, his gaze brilliant and intent. "Definitely not single. I feel trapped in some kind of no-man's-land. I want my wife but she doesn't want me."

Angie swallowed tremulously. "That's not true, Owen. You know it isn't true. I've never said I didn't want you."

He lowered himself slowly on top of her, pushing her into the pillows. His eyes never left hers.

Something primitive and utterly feminine deep inside Angie stirred under the impact of Owen's glittering gaze. She felt her whole body respond to the heavy, sensual weight of him.

"You want me?" Owen asked.

"Yes."

"Show me." Owen threaded his fingers through her hair, anchoring her gently. "Show me you want me, wife. Lord knows I ache for you. I'm going out of my mind with wanting you."

She could read the truth in his eyes. He might not understand love, but tonight Owen could have written the book on frustrated desire. And all that volatile masculine passion was focused on her.

With my body, I thee worship.

Owen was her husband. She loved him. She had never wanted anything or anyone as much as she wanted this man, whom she loved with all her heart.

"Owen," Angie whispered. "Owen, I want you. I have always wanted you. You know that." She saw the flare of response in his eyes. Angie framed his hard face between her palms and brought his lips gently down to hers.

"Angie."

Owen's mouth closed over hers with a desperate hunger that Angie had never before felt in him. In the past there had been passion in Owen's kisses, but it had always been controlled. She had sensed its presence, even had strong hints of its power, but she had never experienced the full force of it. Tonight Owen's passion was a fire storm that would swamp them both.

Owen caught Angie's face between his hands as his mouth ravished hers. He invaded the sweet, vulnerable warmth behind her lips with an intimate aggression that seared her senses. When she started to respond, her fingers clenching around his shoulders, he groaned.

Angie felt Owen lift himself away from her. She started to protest then went still as she felt his fingers on the buttons of her silk blouse.

When she felt him fumble she realized she was not the only one shivering with need. *It's so unlike Owen to be clumsy,* she thought in growing wonder. Somehow, Owen's loss of sensual finesse at this crucial moment charmed her and endeared him to her as nothing else could have done.

"Stupid buttons," Owen muttered. He gave up the task of trying to undo them and yanked at the delicate fabric of the blouse.

Angie bit back a gasp of astonishment as buttons popped and went flying across the room. "Good heavens, Owen."

"It's all right," he assured her roughly as he dropped hot, urgent kisses along her throat. "I'll buy you all the blouses you want, I swear." He stroked her breast, his thumb grazing her nipple. "A hundred blouses. A million blouses. Just let me touch you, sweetheart. I need to touch you like this. Need to feel you." And then his mouth was on her breast.

Angie sucked in her breath, her fingers biting into Owen's shoulders. She arched herself against him as his hand moved across her stomach to the curve of her hip.

"Yes, love. Yes. It's going to be so good, Angie. So good." Owen found the fastening of her skirt, made one or two attempts to undo it and abandoned the attempt in frustration. His hand swept lower. He found the hem of the skirt and shoved the entire mass of fabric up to her waist.

Angie shuddered when she felt his fingers on the inside of her thigh. She started panting when he parted her legs with one of his own. His trousers were excitingly rough against her skin. She realized vaguely that she was clutching at him now, lifting herself, straining for a more intimate touch.

"Angie, tell me again that you want me. *Tell me.*"

"I want you. I want you. I want you." She covered his hard jaw and strong throat with small, hungry little kisses.

Owen groped for and found the waistband of Angie's silken panty hose. He tugged them over her hips and pushed them impatiently along her legs to her ankles. She kicked them off, and when she was free of them, he brought his hand up her leg until he was inches from the hot, damp core of her.

Then, with a low, husky groan, he found her and closed his hand possessively over her.

"Owen. Oh, please, Owen. Please." Angie writhed against his hand. She felt him teasing her with his fingers and thought she would go mad. She clung to him, pleading for more.

Everything was happening so fast, she could no longer think clearly. It was like being caught in a lightning storm.

"Oh, yes, sweetheart. So good. I knew it would be like this. You all hot and soft and clinging." As he spoke, Owen eased one finger into her, his thumb simultaneously gliding over the secret swell of flesh hidden in the dark thatch of hair between her thighs. "You're ready for me. You want this as much as I do."

Angie cried out softly. Every nerve in her body was alive with tension now. She knew Owen felt it. She heard his thick exclamation of satisfaction, then she heard the hiss of his zipper being lowered.

"Owen?" She opened her eyes and looked at him through her lashes. He was watching her face with a fierce intensity.

"Now, sweetheart. Tonight. You're so beautiful, so ready for me. I can't wait any longer to make you my wife."

"Yes."

She closed her eyes and once more her fingers gripped his shoulders as he slowly, deliberately thrust himself into her.

He filled Angie with a steady, relentless pressure that nonetheless made some allowance for her sensitive flesh.

"Am I hurting you?" Owen's brow was damp with sweat.

"No. Never."

Angie trembled as she took him into her. She felt as though she was taking all of him, his strength, his male power, the very essence of Owen Sutherland. Now, in this moment, he belonged to her completely, and she knew beyond a shadow of a doubt that she belonged to him.

When he had buried himself deep within her, Owen trapped her face between his hands. For a timeless moment he looked at her with so much glittering emotion in his eyes that Angie wanted to weep and laugh and cry out with joy.

"Hello, Mrs. Owen Sutherland," Owen whispered. His voice was unbelievably tender but unmistakably laced with male triumph.

She should have been appalled by the satisfaction in his gaze, Angie told herself ruefully. But she was not.

Probably because in addition to the triumph she saw there, she also saw the unshakable promise of commitment.

Owen was giving himself tonight, just as surely as he was claiming her.

And then Owen started to move within her and Angie could no longer think at all. With a soft, choked exclamation, she surrendered to the glittering storm of sensation that swept over her.

ANGIE STIRRED in Owen's arms a while later. She started to turn and realized her skirt was bunched around her waist. She was still wearing her blouse, too. It was open, revealing one breast and only partially concealing the other. Her panty hose lay on the floor beside the bed.

Owen was sprawled beside her, one arm curved possessively around her, the other behind his head. One of his legs was covering hers. She could feel the crisp texture of his trousers against her skin.

Angie looked down the length of their entwined bodies. Owen's zipper was still unzipped. His shirt was half undone. Tantalizing glimpses of crisp, curling dark hair were visible through the openings of both shirt and trousers.

"Sure looks like the shocking aftermath of a scene of unbridled lust, doesn't it?" Owen did not open his eyes.

"Well, yes, as a matter of fact, it does." Angie smiled. "I do feel a bit ravished, now that you mention it."

Owen opened one eye. "This wasn't quite the way I had planned it, you know."

"I know how you had it planned. Champagne, room service and the honeymoon suite. I was there, remember?" Angie slipped her fingers inside his shirt.

"So you were." Owen's mouth curved faintly. He opened both eyes, revealing the lazy satisfaction in his gaze. "Things didn't go according to schedule, but it doesn't matter." He brought his hand along her bare leg. "Everything is just fine now."

"Is it?"

"Uh-huh." He closed his hand around the back of her head and brought her mouth down to his. He kissed her slowly, lingeringly and with a deep, tender possessiveness. "Everything is just perfect. About time, too. You kept me waiting long enough, lady."

"Owen—"

"Hush." He rolled on top of her, trapping her between his hands. "We haven't finished our wedding night yet."

"We haven't?"

"No. But don't worry. This time we'll do things with a little more class. Hell, this time, I'll even take off my pants first."

THE NEXT TIME Angie stirred and stretched in Owen's arms, she realized he was wide awake, studying the darkened ceiling. She sensed the change in his mood.

"Owen? Is something wrong?"

His arm tightened around her reassuringly. "No, honey. I was just thinking, that's all."

"About what? Us?"

"No."

Angie made a face in the shadows. "Thanks a lot."

He turned his head, looking at her in surprise. "What do you mean by that? Why should I be thinking about us? Things are okay now. We've finally got this marriage on track. Everything's settled between us."

"Oh, I see. Everything's settled. Just like that?"

He wound his fingers in her hair and tugged gently. "Kiss me."

She obliged, leaning down to brush her mouth across his. He nipped playfully at her lower lip, then caught and held her close for a deeper kiss.

"Like I said," Owen murmured. "Everything's settled between us. What I was thinking about was something you said earlier out on the terrace."

"The something that turned you from a civilized gentleman into a caveman?"

He ignored that. "About offering Langley a job."

"Oh, that."

"Yeah. That. What was it all about, Angie?"

"You'll probably lose your temper all over again if I try to explain," she said.

"Try anyway."

"All right, here goes. I think you should offer Glen a good position with the company. You could do it. You have the power to hire anyone you want at a high level."

"Give me one good reason I should offer Langley a high level position."

"I'll give you three good reasons. The first two are Celia and your sister, Kim. They would both appreciate it more than you know. They already feel rejected enough by the terms of your father's will. Your rejection of Kim's husband has added to that feeling. Making an offer to Glen would reassure both Kim and Celia that you at least respect their wishes—that you care about them. It would be a nice gesture, Owen."

"You don't run a company like Sutherland Hotels with nice gestures."

"One nice gesture isn't going to hurt. You can afford this one."

"You said there were three good reasons I should make Langley an offer. What was the third reason?"

Angie smiled as she readied her *coup de grace*. "You can make your grand gesture with perfect safety. Glen's going to turn you down."

"He's going to *what?*"

"You heard me. Glen has no intention of working for you. I can't blame him, either. I think you'd probably be a terrible boss. But that's beside the point. He's had an excellent offer from an engineering firm in Seattle and he intends to take it."

"If that's so," Owen said, sounding suspicious, "why should I go through the charade of making him an offer?"

"I've told you, for Celia and Kim's sake. Glen says Kim is tearing herself apart because you won't show some sign of being willing to accept her husband."

"Why should that bother her?" Owen muttered.

"Because you're her big brother, of course. It's perfectly natural that she would want your approval. I'm a little sister, Owen. I know what I'm talking about. Glen wants you to make the gesture for Kim's sake. Then he will very nicely decline and take the Seattle job."

"Langley told you this?"

"Yes. Tonight, when we were talking on the sofa."

"And you believed him?"

Angie got the first inkling that her suggestion was being met with some skepticism. She frowned. "Of course I believed him. Why would Glen lie to me?"

"To get you to do exactly what you are doing, maybe?"

Angie was immediately incensed. "Owen, how can you say such a thing?"

"Easy. I've had a little more experience with men like Langley than you've had, honey. You've led a sheltered life. It's only natural that you'd be a bit gullible. Unfortunately, it looks like Kim has the same problem. She fell for Langley's line, too."

Angie sat up, angry all over again. "Tell me the truth, Owen. Do you have any real evidence that Glen married your sister because of her connection to Sutherland Hotels, or are you just suspicious of him on general principles?"

"I don't need hard evidence. Just look at the facts. The guy swept her off her feet with a whirlwind courtship. They were married less than three months after they first met. Two months later Kim is hounding me to give Langley a position with Sutherland. You tell me if that doesn't sound suspicious."

"A whirlwind courtship, hmm?" Angie smiled slowly. "Three months, you say? That's just about as much of a courtship as I got, isn't it?"

Owen scowled. "Don't try to draw any comparisons here, Angie. It's not the same situation at all."

Angie pursed her lips thoughtfully. "Let's see, a mere three-month courtship and right after the wedding we discover the groom has some serious interest in the bride's family business. Very suspicious situation, if you ask me. I can certainly see why you were alarmed. In fact, I know exactly how you feel."

"Damn it, Angie, don't start. As of tonight I don't want to hear anymore about that."

"Whatever you say, Owen."

He eyed her warily. "That's better." When she did not argue, he smiled slowly and reached for her. "Much better."

OWEN AWOKE shortly before dawn. He lay quietly, relishing the feel of Angie's warm, soft body curled against him. It felt good. Right. The way it was supposed to be. She was his. *His wife.*

He turned his head to study her in the predawn light. Her hair was a tangled wave of fire against the pillow, and her dark copper lashes were closed, concealing her turquoise eyes. Her soft mouth was slightly parted, inviting his kiss, even in sleep. The elusive, womanly scent of her tugged at his insides, arousing him.

Owen considered awakening her so that he could make love to her again. Then he thought about how much she had given him last night. Reluctantly, he decided to play the gentleman and let her sleep.

He certainly had not been much of a gentleman last night, he thought as he eased himself from under the covers. His first night with Angie had not gone according to plan at all. But this morning that no longer mattered. The marriage had been consummated. He and Angie were man and wife.

A surge of euphoric satisfaction hit Owen as he went into the bathroom and turned on the shower. He could not remember the last time he had felt this good. He was laughing silently by the time he finally stepped under the water.

Owen was still grinning twenty minutes later when he loped down the stairs and sauntered into the breakfast room. Betty was setting a pot of coffee and a basket of freshly baked muffins on the table.

"'Morning, sir."

"Good morning, Betty." Owen sat down and picked up the coffeepot. The aroma of freshly ground and brewed beans was terrific. "By the way. A word to the wise. If you want to make it to retirement around here, I suggest that in future you refrain from commenting on my personal habits to others in this household."

Betty smiled complacently. "You can't fire me, Owen Sutherland. I've worked for this family for over thirty years. I remember you from the days when you used to sneak around stacking chairs to make a ladder to get to the cookie jar."

"A touching memory, I'm sure, Betty, but I no longer have to steal my cookies. I just reach out and take them. As many as I want."

"Ruthless, huh? That what you're trying to tell me?" Betty chuckled, obviously unintimidated. "Save your threats, boy. You don't scare me. And if you want to know why I told your sister you and your new bride weren't sharing the same bed, I'll tell you."

"Okay, why did you tell Kim about that?"

Betty grinned widely. "'Cause I knew it'd get back to you in no time, of course. Figured you'd do something about the problem. And it was clear from the look on your face when you came in here a minute ago that you did do something about it last night."

Owen managed a severe scowl. "Your idea of playing Cupid, I take it?"

"Sure. Knew right off something was wrong between you and your missus. I could tell she was head-over-heals in love with you but feelin' kind of uncertain, too. When I realized you weren't even sleepin' together, I decided that was a big part of the problem."

"Is that right?"

"Yep. Thought I'd give you a little shove. Easiest way to shove you is right in the middle of your Sutherland pride."

"Lucky for you I'm in such a good mood this morning, Betty. That's all I can say." Owen picked up a hot muffin, sliced it open and dribbled honey into it.

"A good mood, huh? A good woman does that for a man. And there ain't no doubt you got yourself a mighty good woman." Betty picked up a tray and headed for the door.

Owen decided he had no quarrel with that conclusion. He bit into the muffin. It was perfect. He finished it and reached for another.

Glen Langley strolled through the door, yawning. He eyed the muffin basket as he sat down. "'Morning, Sutherland. You planning on eating all of those muffins yourself?"

"You can have one."

"Gosh, thanks. I guess the lord of the manor is feeling generous this morning." Glen reached for a muffin and poured himself a cup of coffee.

Owen ignored that and munched thoughtfully for a moment. "You really want to work for me?"

Glen blinked in surprise. "Hell, no. No offense, Sutherland, but I think you'd make a miserable boss. What I want from you is a job offer. And I want you to make it in front of Kim."

"Angie says if I make the offer you'll turn it down. What guarantee do I have you'll do that?"

Glen shrugged. "None at all. You'll be making it in front of a witness—namely, your sister. If I change my mind and decide to accept the offer, you'll be stuck with me."

"That's what I'm afraid of."

"I can understand that," Glen said. "You've got good reason to be nervous. Believe me, Sutherland, you may be the world's nastiest CEO, but I can promise you that if I ever came on board as an employee, I would make your life a living hell."

Owen smiled slowly, appreciating the threat. "Yeah, I'll bet you would. Why'd you marry Kim?"

"The usual reasons. Fell in love with her first time I saw her. Realized I'd better grab her fast or I'd lose her. Didn't want to give her too much time to think. Give women enough time to think and they start inventing all sorts of problems that a man has a tough time solving. Know what I mean?"

Owen thought about what he had gone through since his wedding day. He winced. "Yeah, I know what you mean."

"Figured you did. I sized up the situation with Kim and your family and then I went in fast. I knew you were going to be the biggest stumbling block. I swept Kim off her feet and married her before she had a chance to fret too long about getting your approval."

"What made you think I wouldn't approve?"

"You're a big brother, right? Big brothers hardly ever approve of the men who marry their little sisters. Hell, I'm a big brother myself. I know what I'm talking about. On top of that perfectly normal state of affairs, Kim had lost her father two years ago. That meant big brother was going to be playing father figure, too. It would make the test even tougher to pass."

"So you decided to short-circuit the situation with a whirlwind courtship and a quickie marriage."

Glen's eyes met Owen's. "That's about it. Now, of course, I've got to clean up the mess. But at least I've got my wife and I can take my time getting you to see the light."

"Damn," said Owen.

"Yeah, I know. But I think you and I have a lot more in common than you realize, Sutherland. I'd say we tend to operate the same way."

"Go in fast, get the job done and clean up the mess later, is that it?" Owen finished the last of his muffin. He folded his arms and rested them on the table.

"Isn't that what you're doing right now?" Glen asked quietly. "Cleaning up a mess? From what I've heard, you don't spend much time here at Jade Lake if you can help it. The fact that you brought your bride where you knew she wouldn't be welcome means you've got a drastic situation on your hands. Probably something to do with the merger. Am I getting warm?"

Owen said nothing.

"I'll make a deal with you, Sutherland. Make me an offer, a good one. I'll turn it down and then I'll take Kim away from here. It'll give you one less thing to worry about."

"What if she won't go with you, Langley?" Owen asked softly. "Kim wants you to go to work in the hotel business. So does her mother."

"That's a risk I've got to take. I'm banking on the fact that she loves me and she knows I love her. I think she'll trust her future to me."

Owen swore softly and sat back. He shoved his hands into his pockets and stretched his legs out under the table. Langley was tough. Tougher than Owen realized. Angie's judgment of the situation had been accurate, after all.

She didn't know much about the hotel business, but he was beginning to acknowledge she might know a lot more about what made families tick than he did.

He was still pondering that and Glen was still drinking coffee when Kim wandered in a few minutes later. She went straight to her husband and kissed him lightly before she sat down and helped herself to coffee.

"Good morning, Owen," Kim said coolly.

"Hello, Kim."

"You certainly made a spectacle of yourself last night."

Owen decided his mood was still too good to be ruined this early in the morning. "I married a Townsend. Townsends tend to get exuberant when they get excited. We Sutherlands, on the other hand, are a touchy bunch. We tend to get mad as hell when someone offends our pride, don't we?"

Kim eyed him uncertainly. "What are you talking about, Owen?"

"Never mind." Owen made up his mind. "I was just about to offer your husband, here, a position as vice president of engineering with Sutherland and Townsend. He can go straight to work in the head office planning our first hotel in the South Pacific. There will be some travel involved as the planning stage moves into the construction phase, but you can go with him."

Kim's fork clattered to her plate. "Owen, are you serious?" She stared at him in astonishment. "You mean it?"

Owen met and held Langley's eyes. "You know me, Kim. I never say anything I don't mean. The job is Glen's, if he wants it. Something tells me he'll work out just fine at Sutherland and Townsend."

"Owen, this is wonderful. I know you won't regret it." Kim jumped to her feet, darted around the table and threw her arms around Owen. "Thank you, Owen. Thank you so much."

Owen realized there were tears shining in his sister's eyes. He smiled faintly. "Hey, it's okay, kid. Least I can do for a member of the family, right?"

"Right." Kim laughed. She released Owen and went happily to her seat. "This is perfect, isn't it, Glen?"

"Yeah," Glen said. "Just perfect. Except for one small fact."

Kim frowned. "What fact?"

"I've got a better offer in Seattle. And the truth is, I'd rather work on aircraft control systems than on hotel air-conditioning and plumbing systems. I'm grateful to your brother, but I'm going to turn down his offer."

"But, Glen—"

Owen overrode Kim's protest. "The offer's good, Langley," he said quietly. "I wouldn't have made it otherwise. Like I said a minute ago, I always mean what I say."

Glen smiled. "I know. I appreciate it. But I think it'll be better if Kim and I go to Seattle."

Owen got to his feet. "I hear you. You and Kim talk it out. Whatever you decide is fine with me. See you later."

It was a beautiful day, Owen thought as he left the house and walked into the morning sunshine. He did not recall Jade Lake ever looking quite this shade of emerald green. Even the mountains seemed more picturesque this morning. Not quite so dark and forbidding. For once the atmosphere around Jade Lake wasn't making him claustrophobic.

Owen glanced at the window of the master bedroom. It was open. He saw Angie leaning out, taking in the sight of the lake. She was wearing her quilted robe, sleep-tousled hair swirled around her shoulders. When she saw him watching her, she smiled and blew him a kiss.

Owen grinned and waved at her. He could see her blush even from where he stood.

He started to whistle as he sauntered down the path to the boat house to see what Jeffers was doing.

8

CELIA WAS ALONE in the breakfast room when Angie arrived. She was standing at the window, gazing at the boat house while she absently stirred her coffee.

"Good morning, Celia." Angie poured herself a cup of coffee.

"Good morning, Angie." Celia turned slowly. She smiled uneasily. "I suspect we have you to thank for Owen's sudden change of heart."

Angie hovered over the muffin basket, dithering between blueberry and bran. "What change of heart?"

"Kim tells me he offered Glen a position with Sutherland Hotels. A good position."

"Did he?" Angie decided on the blueberry muffin. "Don't thank me. I didn't have anything to do with it."

"I have a hard time believing that, Angie. Owen is one of the most stubborn men I have ever met. Takes after his father." Celia's smile turned wry. "Once he makes a decision, he almost never changes his mind. His Sutherland pride won't allow it. But this morning he seems to have done exactly that."

Angie bit into her muffin. "Owen is stubborn, but he's not completely unreasonable."

"Perhaps unreasonable is the wrong word. Implacable might be better."

Angie grinned around a mouthful of muffin. "Or intractable? How about impossible? Imperious? Immovable? Occasionally even a touch idiotic?"

"You find this all very amusing, don't you?" Celia asked quietly.

"Not really. I'm sorry if I seem facetious, Celia. Another annoying Townsend trait, no doubt."

Celia looked at her for a long moment. "No doubt. Be that as it may, I owe you my thanks for patching up things between Owen and Kim. It was very painful watching their relationship being torn apart. Of course Kim did rush into marriage with Glen, and his motives did appear suspect for a time. But I knew Kim loved him and after I got to know Glen, I felt he was an honest young man who cared deeply for my daughter."

"I happen to agree with you. I like Glen."

"I thought once Owen got a chance to know Glen, he would come to accept him. But then Kim came up with the notion of Glen going to work for Sutherland Hotels and Owen exploded."

"It was probably Kim's way of trying to force Owen to accept her husband," Angie mused. "Nobody forces Owen to do anything."

"Very true." Celia sighed. "I assure you, he was just as stubborn and unreachable when he was a boy. Owen was thirteen years old when I married his father. And he already considered himself an adult. The boy never did accept me as his mother. Oh, he was always polite, mind you. Always well-behaved. But there was a distance between us. He was cool and self-contained, even as a boy."

"I can't see Owen as a little boy."

"Neither can I," Celia admitted. "He was certainly not a little boy when I first came into his life. More like a younger version of his father in many ways. From the day I met him, he made it quietly clear that he knew he was being groomed to take charge of Sutherland Hotels and the Sutherland family. You could see that he had accepted the responsibilities before he even knew what they would entail."

"And the last thing he wanted was a new mother, right?" Angie asked gently.

Celia put down her coffee cup. "Precisely. As I said, he was always polite to me, but he never saw me as his mother. I think that to Owen, I have never been anything but one more responsibility he was expected to eventually shoulder. And he has done his duty by me, I'll grant him that. He has done his duty by all of us. One thing you can say about Owen, he fulfills his responsibilities. In his own arrogant way."

Angie heard an old, sad regret in Celia's voice. She was searching for the right words with which to respond when Kim breezed through the door, followed by Glen. Kim looked happier and more lovely than Angie had yet seen her.

"Hi, Angie. There you are, Mom. I came to tell you that Glen and I will be leaving soon. There's no point staying. We've talked it over and I realize that he would much rather work in the aircraft industry than the hotel business. He's had the most wonderful offer from a firm in Seattle, haven't you, darling?"

Glen smiled at his glowing wife. "I think it will be a good job. And I think Kim will like Seattle."

"I'm going to love Seattle," Kim assured everyone.

Derwin appeared in the doorway, his bushy white brows locked in a deep scowl. "What the devil is going on here? I heard Owen offered you a vice presidency, Glen. Is that true?"

"It's true," Glen said easily. "But I've turned him down."

Derwin stared at him. "Turned him down? You can't be serious."

"Afraid so." Glen looked at his watch then at Kim. "We'd better get packed, honey. Your brother's going to take us across the lake so we can pick up the car. Got a long drive home ahead of us."

"Don't worry. I can be ready in half an hour." Kim turned to Angie and smiled. "Thank you, Angie. I know you had a hand in this. That brother of mine can be so darned stubborn."

"I think he was just feeling a little overprotective," Angie murmured. "I've seen the same syndrome in my own brother, Harry. Big brothers get that way about their little sisters, I guess."

Kim tilted her head thoughtfully. "Maybe you're right. I never thought of it that way. I just assumed Owen was being his usual arrogant self." She went across the room and gave Angie a quick hug. "You know, I think it's going to be interesting having you in the family."

"Thank you," Angie said, surprised and touched by the unexpected show of warmth.

Glen laughed softly. "Something tells me things are going to be a little different around here from now on. See you at the next family reunion, Angie." He came forward and gave her a quick, affectionate hug. "And thanks," he murmured. "I owe you."

"No," Angie said quickly, but Glen was not listening. With a nod to Celia and Derwin, he took Kim's hand and tugged her toward the door.

Derwin's scowl deepened as the pair left the breakfast room. "I can't believe that boy turned down a decent offer with Sutherland Hotels."

"I think it was for the best," Celia said. "A young couple should stand on their own feet right after marriage. Gives them a sense of independence. All Kim really wanted was to know that Owen accepted Glen. She's satisfied. And that's what counts, don't you think, Derwin?"

"I was never offered a vice presidency," Derwin growled. "I was never even offered a job in the damn mail room." He turned to confront Angie. "This is your doing, isn't it?"

"Now, Derwin," Celia began quietly.

"It is her doing. And I, for one, would like to know what is going on around here. We all witnessed that caveman spectacle Owen put on for us last night. I've never seen anything so undignified in my life. Typical of a Townsend, perhaps, but totally out of character for Owen. She's doing things to him. Changing him."

"Please, Derwin," Celia said.

He ignored her, still glowering ferociously at Angie. "You've seduced Owen, that's what you've done. You caused that boy to make a fool of himself in front of his own family. And now you're starting to interfere in family matters. You're up to something. I know it."

"*Derwin*," Celia snapped, "I think that's quite enough."

"My guess is it hasn't even begun." Derwin threw down his napkin and stalked to the door. "Never could trust Townsends. They're always scheming. Always using people. You'll see, Celia. Mark my words. Owen will live to regret the day he married a Townsend. He'll learn his lesson the hard way."

An uncomfortable silence descended on the breakfast room. Celia smiled apologetically. "I'm sorry, Angie. Derwin and Helen are rather set in their ways. Old habits die hard, and they have been in the habit of hating Townsends for a very long time."

"I wish I knew why," Angie said. She met Celia's eyes. "Do you?"

Celia shook her head. "No, not really. I just know it all goes back to the first merger attempt between the two companies. I wasn't married to Owen's father then so I don't know the details. Whatever happened left a bad taste in everyone's mouth, apparently. I'll admit that out of loyalty to the family, I've been as suspicious of Townsends as everyone else, although you're the first one I've actually met."

"We're quite lovable when you get to know us."

Before Celia could respond to that Owen came through the door.

His eyes found his stepmother first. "'Morning, Celia. Seen Angie?" Then he spotted Angie at the table. His eyes gleamed. "Ah, there you are, honey. I've been looking for you. I've got to run Kim and Glen across the lake in a few minutes. While I'm gone why don't you have Betty make us up another picnic lunch? We'll take the boat out this afternoon and we'll hit a couple of the islands at the south end of the lake."

"All right," Angie said. "How long will you be gone?"

"After I see Kim and Glen on their way, I'm going to pick up some supplies Jeffers ordered at the hardware store." Owen shrugged. "I shouldn't be gone more than a couple of hours."

"Fine." Angie felt herself blushing under the expression in Owen's eyes. She knew very well he intended to make love to her on one of those islands at the south end of the lake. Hot memories of the previous night flooded her, making her senses dance with expectation.

"See you." Owen started for the door.

"Owen?" Celia called him quietly.

He turned. "Yeah?"

"Thank you," Celia said quietly.

"For what? Offering Langley a job? Forget it. No big deal. He turned me down, anyway."

"It meant a lot to Kim. And to me."

Owen hesitated, then his mouth curved faintly. "Langley's okay. Dad would've liked him. Guy's got guts."

MUCH LATER that afternoon Owen anchored the launch in a tiny cove on one of the miniature islands that dotted the south end of Jade Lake. He glanced at Angie, who was eyeing the short walk to shore.

"It's not very deep. Just roll up your jeans and take off your shoes," Owen advised. "Unless you want me to carry you ashore?"

"I think I can manage. You take the lunch." Angie handed him the basket. Then she kicked off her loafers.

Owen rolled up his jeans. Then he went over the side with the basket in one hand, his shoes in the other. He stood knee deep in the clear water and watched as Angie gingerly swung one bare leg over the edge of the boat.

A rush of pleasure went through him as he vividly recalled the feel of that soft, curving leg against his own last night. He could hardly wait to make love to his wife again.

Angie glanced up at that instant, and she must have seen the warm anticipation in his eyes because she blushed furiously. She looked down quickly, concentrating on her footing. Owen saw the flash of gold on her hand as the sun glinted on her wedding ring, and a hot, possessive feeling surged through him.

"I thought we came here for lunch." Angie splashed into the water and waded ashore.

"Lunch and other forms of nourishment." Owen swung the picnic basket, feeling lighthearted and curiously content with life. "Besides, it's not lunch, it's a midafternoon snack. Too late for lunch."

"Thanks to the fact that you were over an hour late getting back from Jade," Angie reminded him.

"There's something about hardware stores," Owen said. "Once I get into one, I suddenly think of all kinds of stuff I need. And I don't even like to tinker the way my uncle does. Hell, I don't even have to do my own household repairs."

"Must be a male thing. I've seen my father and brother in a hardware store. It's not a pretty sight." She reached the small, pebbly beach and stood gazing at a fern-choked grotto. "This, on the other hand, is a lovely sight."

"Lovely," Owen agreed, watching the way the sunlight gleamed on Angie's red hair, turning it to fire. He wondered if he could get away with making love to her before he fed her or if she'd insist on eating first. He decided to try his luck. "How about that spot right over there?"

"Okay." Angie plucked the checkered cloth out of the basket and arranged it in a small clearing among the ferns. She sat in the shade of a tree and began unpacking the lunch. "Betty certainly outdid herself this time. Pâté, French bread and a bottle of wine."

Owen grinned as he sprawled on the cloth beside Angie. "She probably wanted to promote the romantic element. Can't blame her." He put his hand on Angie's thigh, squeezing gently. "I'm feeling kind of romantic, myself."

Angie laughed. "You mean you're feeling sexy."

"What's the difference?" Owen slid his hand a little higher up her jeaned thigh. She felt warm and soft, even through the denim. He bent his head and kissed her knee. When he looked into her eyes he saw the wealth of emotion there. He smiled encouragingly, sensing she was about to tell him she loved him.

"Did you get those supplies?" Angie asked as she unwrapped the pâté.

"Huh?" Owen frowned, surprised by the unexpected change of topic.

"Those supplies you said Jeffers asked you to pick up at the hardware store in Jade. Were they in?"

"Oh, yeah. Those. I got them." He watched as she industriously spread pâté on a slice of French bread. "Angie, I'm really not that hungry right now."

"Aren't you?"

"No." He gently removed the slice of bread and the knife from her hands, put them into the basket then reached for her. "Come here, wife."

"I'm here," she whispered.

"Closer." He eased her down onto the checkered cloth and slid his leg between her thighs. She put her arms around him and watched him from beneath lowered lashes. Her smile was soft and inviting, telling him in that timeless, feminine way that she was his. Owen felt his whole body tighten with desire.

"Owen?"

"It's all right. This time we've got privacy. No one can see us from the water."

Owen lowered his mouth to cover Angie's. The picnic lunch was forgotten, and a very short time later she was lying naked and soft beneath him and he was buried deep in her feminine heat. He could feel her clinging to him, feel her tightening deliciously around him. Her nails were digging into his shoulders.

Owen lifted his head to watch hungrily as Angie shivered in his arms the way the sunlight shimmered on the surface of Jade Lake. Her soft cries of sensual fulfillment were the most incredibly exciting sounds Owen had ever heard. He was poised on the brink of his own pounding satisfaction when he vaguely realized he was waiting for something.

But the tiny, delicious contractions deep within Angie's body pulled Owen inevitably into the storm. He forgot why he had been waiting, forgot why he had been holding back a moment earlier. He surrendered to the hot whirlwind with a hoarse exclamation of triumph and pleasure.

It was not until after he shuddered and eventually lay still, his body still damp with perspiration, that Owen remembered what he had been waiting to hear in those final seconds of lovemaking.

He had been waiting to hear Angie tell him she loved him. He frowned slightly as he realized she had not done so since he had started making love to her. But he was too relaxed to worry about it now. He closed his eyes and let himself drift into a state of deep lethargy....

Owen did not realize he had fallen asleep until he awakened some time later to the sound of Angie rustling around in the picnic basket. He opened his eyes and saw that she had already dressed and gone back to the task of spreading pâté on French bread. This time the pâté and bread combination looked great. Owen decided he was ravenously hungry.

"I could eat about half a dozen of those," he said. He got to his feet, pulled on his jeans and went to wash his hands in the lake water.

"I've got a head start on you. Better hurry if you want your fair share." Angie handed him a slice of bread covered with a thick chunk of the pâté.

Owen downed it in two bites. "I'll open the wine." He busied himself with the corkscrew Betty had remembered to provide. "Angie?"

"Um?"

"I've been thinking."

"I've warned you before about that."

He grinned, feeling too lazy and too satisfied to take offense. "How about we go finish this honeymoon someplace else?" He poured the wine into two glasses and handed her one.

"I thought you wanted me here where I couldn't do any damage to the stock offering."

"Hell, that never really entered into it," he admitted. "I knew I could keep the press and anyone else away from you at one of the hotels. I'm the boss, remember?"

Angie slowly lowered her slice of French bread, her eyes never leaving his face. "Then why did you insist we come here?"

"I had this wild idea that if you saw me surrounded by the rest of the Sutherlands, you'd feel obliged to come to my defense." He grinned. "You're the sort who naturally champions the underdog. I thought if you saw the way things are between me and my family, you'd get over being mad and start remembering how you really felt about me."

"I see."

"Matters didn't go quite the way I had planned," Owen admitted. "But everything worked out." He slanted her a deliberate look. "And you do remember now how you really feel about me, don't you, Angie?"

Angie drew up her knees and wrapped her arms around them. Her expression was thoughtful. "You want this marriage to work, don't you, Owen?"

"Damn right, I do."

She nodded. "So do I."

He smiled with deep satisfaction. "I know. I've known it all along. You just needed time to get over your anger. And your fear that you'd been used. Some of the problem was my own fault. Maybe I didn't give you a chance to get to know me well enough before the marriage. I rushed you. If there'd been more time, you'd have been more secure with me."

"I think you're right. I feel I know you much better now, Owen," Angie's expression was intent and serious.

"You can say that again." He leaned over, kissed her soundly and smiled. "I was hoping that after we'd turned this marriage into a normal one, you'd come to exactly that conclusion."

"You're very sure of yourself, aren't you, Owen?"

He laughed softly. "I'm not going to answer that. It's one of those no-win questions. But if it's any consolation, you did manage to throw a monkey wrench into most of my big plans for the perfect honeymoon. But now I think we can get this wedding trip back on line, don't you?"

"All right."

"Is that all you can say?" He gave her a mocking glance. "Don't tell me you actually like it here at Jade Lake?"

"I won't tell you that. But I will tell you I've learned more about you in the past few days than I learned in the three months before we arrived here, Owen."

That annoyed him. "That's not true, damn it. You just came to your senses here, that's all."

"If you say so."

Owen realized his good mood was starting to evaporate. "Angie, what is it with you? Are you mad or something?"

"No, I'm not mad. I've just been doing a lot of thinking." She rested her chin on her folded knees. "We both agree we want to give this marriage a chance."

"I didn't say that," he muttered. "I said it was going to work. Period."

She nodded in acquiescence. "I think there's a good possibility it will."

"A *possibility?*"

"Yes, the way I see it, we've got a lot going for us. There's a strong physical attraction, for one thing."

"That's for damn sure." Owen took a swallow of his wine.

"And there's that strong business connection between us, too, especially now that Sutherland and Townsend have merged. I was angry at first, but now I've come to the conclusion that having business interests in common could be a binding element in our relationship."

Owen lost his temper at that comment. "Damn it, Angie, our mutual business interests have got nothing to do with this relationship!"

"Yes, they do, Owen." Angie's voice was very calm, very soothing, as if she was dealing with a recalcitrant child. "You can't deny it. You said yourself that we would never have met if it hadn't been for the fact that our families are both in the hotel business. Don't worry, I'm beginning to see it as a strong point in our marriage."

"Angie, will you just give it a rest?"

She gave him an innocent look. "Why are you getting so upset, Owen? I'm telling you what you want to hear, aren't I?"

"I do not want to hear about the business aspect of this marriage," he said through his teeth. *What game does she think she's playing now?* he wondered. "The hotel business is not what is going to hold us together."

"What will hold us together, Owen?"

"All kinds of things."

"Physical attraction? I already mentioned that."

"Not just physical attraction," he growled. "Affection. Mutual respect, mutual interests." *Your love for me,* he shouted silently.

"I mentioned mutual interests, too. The hotel business."

"Not just the hotel business."

She smiled, humoring him. "All right. Picnics. We do seem to have a mutual interest in picnics."

"There's more. A lot more."

"Like what?" she prompted gently.

Owen felt as if he was being driven into a corner. "Trust. Commitment. A sense of responsibility."

"Yes, I think you're right. Those are all wonderful things. Valuable things. Precious things."

"Damn right." *And none of them are as wonderful or as valuable or as precious as your love for me,* he thought savagely. *Why aren't you saying the words, Angie? Why aren't you telling me how much you love me? We're married now. Really married. But you haven't said the words since we became lovers.*

"Owen? Is something wrong?"

"What could be wrong?" He smiled grimly. "I'm alone on an island with the woman I . . ."

"Yes, Owen?"

Owen looked at her and finally saw the soft, anxious, distinctly hopeful expression in her clear turquoise eyes. It hit him. He knew now what she was doing. Unfortunately for Angie, he could read her like a book. If she thought she could manipulate him this easily into vowing his undying love, she could think again.

Nobody manipulated Owen Sutherland. Not ever. A man who allowed himself to be manipulated was weak. His father had taught him that.

"I'm alone on an island with the woman to whom I happen to be married," Owen said smoothly. "An extremely convenient state of affairs, wouldn't you say?" He reached for her and pulled her on top of his chest.

The sunlight glowed in Angie's hair and the sweet, sexy weight of her thighs against his was already arousing Owen. He forgot his anger over her futile attempt to control him the moment he captured her mouth.

He was alone on an island with his wife and his wife loved him as no other woman had ever loved him. Owen was certain of it, even if she was too proud to admit it at the moment.

He understood pride. He could wait. Angie was much too soft and gentle and too in love with him to hold out for long. She would surrender first in this small undeclared battle she had instigated.

SHE UNDERSTOOD PRIDE, Angie told herself the next morning as she started out on yet another walk around Jade Lake Island. She could wait.

She stopped amid a stand of fir and watched the Sutherland launch skim across the lake toward town. The boat's wake cut a clean swath across the green water. Owen had left a few minutes earlier to exchange one of the parts he had picked up yesterday for Jeffers at the hardware store.

Angie suspected that Jeffers could have handled the task but Owen had obviously been looking for an excuse to get off the island. He had volunteered to take the launch to town.

Angie knew Owen was getting restless. It was time to leave. He had started to talk about finishing the honeymoon elsewhere yesterday but she had sidetracked him with her puny attempt to get him to admit he loved her.

Her mouth curved downward at the memory of how her efforts to force him to recognize his love for her had backfired. So much for the subtle approach. The man was as stubborn as a mule. Maybe she should get herself a stick and thump him between the ears until she got his full attention, she mused.

It was clear Owen was content to wallow in her love for him—equally clear he had no intention of dealing with such dangerously soft emotions in himself. Owen, indeed the whole Sutherland family, seemed uncomfortable with intense emotions.

It was easy enough to see why Owen was so reluctant to admit to his own feelings. Angie had learned enough about him since she had come to Jade Lake to understand where the problem lay. As a boy he had lost his mother before he had ever really known her. He had been raised by a father who had no doubt encouraged such solid, masculine traits as willpower, the ability to command others and arrogant authority—all characteristics that had served Owen well in his role as heir to the throne of the Sutherland empire.

Celia had come into Owen's life much too late to effect any real change. Owen's path had been clearly marked by the time he was thirteen. In any event, Celia had soon found herself busy with a child of her own and had been content to let Owen continue to grow up under his father's guidance.

Helen and Derwin were clearly too bitter about their own roles in the Sutherland hierarchy to waste much affection on the boy who would be taking his father's place . . . the boy on whom they would someday be dependent for their income and position in the Sutherland corporation. The boy whom they must have resented even then, on some level.

Angie turned at the sound of footsteps approaching. Derwin was striding briskly through the fallen pine needles. He appeared to be in a hurry.

"Good morning, Angie." Derwin nodded coolly. "Pleasant day."

"Yes, it is."

"I see Owen is underway. Heard him say he planned to go over to Jade this morning." Derwin peered across the water at the wake of the small launch. "Don't imagine he'll be back for a couple of hours."

"Probably not. He was mumbling something about crescent wrenches and valve fittings when I saw him off a few minutes ago." Angie smiled. "I have no doubt but that once he gets into that hardware store, he'll think of all kinds of interesting things to check out."

"No doubt." Derwin's thick brows drew together in a frown as he continued to stare out over the lake. "Well, now, I wonder who this is coming toward us."

"Who?" Angie turned to face the lake again and saw that the small boat Derwin had noticed was slowing as it neared Jade Lake Island.

A young man who could not have been out of his teens waved to get their attention. Then he cupped his hands around his mouth.

"I've got a message for Mrs. Sutherland."

"I'm Mrs. Sutherland," Angie called back.

"From a guy who says he works for your brother. He says it's important. Wants to see you right away. Asked me to give you a lift across the lake."

A sudden, overwhelming fear enveloped Angie. "I'll meet you at the dock," she shouted.

She started to run toward the boat house.

9

"SAID HIS NAME was Rawlings and that he worked for Harry and Palmer Townsend. That's all I know, ma'am." The teenager, a thin young man dressed in jeans and a T-shirt, squinted at Angie from the boat. "He asked me to come over here and get you. Said he needs to talk to you right away. Said nobody would take his phone calls here at the Sutherland place."

Angie glanced at Derwin, who stood beside her on the dock. "Do you know anything about any phone calls from a Mr. Rawlings?"

Derwin grimaced dourly. "No. But Betty was instructed to refer all calls to Owen, if you will remember. The rest of us aren't even allowed to answer the phone in our own home anymore."

Angie recalled Owen's instructions to his family. All phone calls were to be directed to him and no one outside the clan was allowed ashore without an invitation. She had assumed all that had changed since the night she and Owen had made love.

But now that Angie thought about it she realized she had never heard Owen revoke his orders. Why should he have altered the rules, she thought grimly. Nothing had really changed between them, had it?

Of course it had. If the big, stubborn, arrogant idiot didn't realize that, he could darn well figure it out for himself!

"I'll come with you to see this Rawlings," Angie said to the teenager. "Can you bring me back across the lake?"

"Sure."

"Okay." Angie climbed into the boat. "Derwin, please tell the others I'll be back shortly."

"Very well."

As the boat sped away from the dock, Angie glanced back and saw Derwin staring after it. The craft was halfway across the lake before she saw him turn around and start up the path to the main house. She looked at the young man who was piloting the boat.

"What did you say your name was?" Angie called out above the roar of the engine.

"Dave. Dave Markel. My family owns that house over there to the left of town. I work at the marina."

Angie brushed wind-whipped hair out of her eyes. "Lived here long?"

"All my life. Be leaving this fall, though. Going off to college."

"Congratulations."

"Thanks." Dave grinned. "I'm looking forward to getting out of this burg, I can tell you."

Angie grinned. "I suppose you've known the Sutherlands ever since you were born?"

Dave shrugged. "Just to say hello to if I see one of 'em on the street. They don't socialize around here much. Kind of standoffish, if you know what I mean. At least the older ones are. Don't see much of the head honcho who runs the hotel company or his sister. Didn't even know Owen Sutherland had gotten married until this Rawlings guy showed up and asked if I knew you."

"When did he show up? Rawlings, I mean."

"Don't know when he got into town. But he came down to the marina about an hour ago and said he was looking for someone who could take a message across the lake. Maybe pick you up and bring you back, if you were willing."

Angie realized she was not going to get much more information out of Dave. She sat back in her seat and watched as the marina grew larger on the horizon.

Soon, the outboard bumped against the marina dock and Dave bounded up to assist Angie out of the craft. She glanced around expectantly. The Sutherland launch was tied up a few yards away. There was no sign of Owen.

"Where is this Mr. Rawlings?"

"In the marina café." Dave angled his chin in the direction of a ramshackle little restaurant at the end of the pier. "Said he was going to have a cup of coffee while he waited for you."

"Thanks." Angie walked down the dock, climbed the small flight of steps that led to the shore path and headed for the café.

It was not at all difficult to pick Rawlings out of the crowd at the small burger and coffee joint. He was the only one wearing a tie. It was silk and it went very nicely with his expensive suit.

Angie eyed him curiously as she walked toward him. Rawlings appeared to be in his mid-thirties. Dark-haired and dark-eyed, he had the alert, aggressive look of a man on the way up. He got to his feet as Angie approached.

"Mrs. Sutherland?"

"Yes."

"I'm Jack Rawlings. Please sit down."

Angie slid into the booth across from him. "Is something wrong, Mr. Rawlings? The boy who brought your message said you worked for my brother."

Rawlings flashed her a charming smile. "Not exactly. I admit I told the young man that, but only because I wanted to talk to you in a hurry and I couldn't think of any other way to reach you. I tried calling, but no one returned my calls."

"I see." Angie frowned. "Who are you exactly, Mr. Rawlings, and why did you want to see me?"

Rawlings pushed aside his coffee cup and folded his arms on the plastic tabletop. He fixed her with an intent gaze. "Mrs. Sutherland, I'll be frank. I represent a group of investors who are interested in acquiring a large block of shares in Sutherland and Townsend when it goes public."

"What's that got to do with me?"

"To be perfectly blunt, there have been some unsettling rumors to the effect that your marriage to Sutherland was pure hype. The gossip on the street is that the merger isn't going to work for long. People are saying the old feud is as strong as ever and that Owen Sutherland won't be able to patch things up for more than a year or so."

Angie froze. "That's ridiculous. Where on earth did you hear that?"

Rawlings shrugged. "Street gossip, like I said. Please understand, Mrs. Sutherland. My people are preparing to put a lot of money on the line. If the Sutherland and Townsend merger is shaky from the start and management is going to be bickering constantly because of the old feud, my investors stand to lose a great deal of cash."

"You brought me here to find out if my marriage is solid so you could figure out if the merger is solid?" Angie asked incredulously.

"Let's just say I'm looking for a little clarification. If your marriage to Sutherland was nothing more than a publicity gimmick, then, yes, my people are going to be concerned about just how secure the merger itself is. I'm told the feud between the two companies left a lot of bad blood on both sides."

Angie was furious. "That's ridiculous."

"Look," Rawlings said with an ingratiating smile, "You see my problem, don't you? If those feelings are still strong, they're bound to affect management. And bad management of Sutherland and Townsend will adversely affect my group's investment."

Angie slipped out of the booth and got to her feet. "I certainly do see your problem, Mr. Rawlings. Your problem is that you listen to gossip. I can assure you that in this case, your inside information is wrong. I am very much married to Owen Sutherland. Furthermore, I resent your lying in order to get me to meet you here. If that is the way your group of investors works, then as far as I'm concerned, I don't particularly want them putting money into my family's company."

"Take it easy, Mrs. Sutherland." Rawlings hurried out of the booth when he realized she was turning on her heel to leave. He started after her. "I was just trying to find out what was going on."

Angie refused to turn. She was striding toward the door of the café when it opened.

Owen strode into the restaurant. His gaze found her immediately then went to the man who was following her. Angie saw the cold flames leap in Owen's eyes.

Owen took two long strides forward, reached out and caught Angie's arm. He pulled her close. "What's going on here?"

"This is Mr. Rawlings," Angie said quickly. "He represents some investors who are interested in the Sutherland and Townsend stock."

"I know who he is." Owen pinned Angie to his side as he confronted Jack Rawlings. "If you've got any questions, you can talk to me, Rawlings. My wife does not get involved with the family business."

"Hey, give me a break, Sutherland. I'm just trying to do my job. You know that. This is just business."

"The hell it is. I'm on my honeymoon. I'm not interested in talking business at the moment." Owen flashed Angie an intimate smile that did not quite wipe out the seething anger in his eyes. He flicked his gaze to Rawlings. "And for the record, I don't like the way you do your job, Rawlings. Maybe you and your little group of sharks had better go find more interesting meat."

"Don't give me that, Sutherland," Rawlings said. "My people have a lot of cash to invest. You need them."

"Sutherland and Townsend doesn't need your group and we both know it. The stock is going to be red-hot when it goes public and you're well aware of it. Your efforts to drive down the offering price are useless. Now get out of here before I toss you into the lake."

"Look, I'm acting on solid information. I've got a right to know whether this merger is for real or if you've got potential problems. I've heard a lot of talk that says the old feud isn't dead."

"It's dead, all right." Owen shot Angie another dangerous smile. "Angie and I buried it personally, didn't we, honey?"

Angie felt Owen's fingers biting into her arm. She managed a sweet, wifely expression—the sort of look a woman on her honeymoon was expected to give her husband. "We certainly did, darling."

"The feud is old news," Owen said easily to Rawlings. "There never was all that much to it, anyway. Just a publicity ploy for both companies. It served its purpose in the past, but times have changed. Sutherland Hotels and Townsend Resorts can grow faster together."

"That's not the way I heard it," Rawlings muttered.

Owen shrugged. "Then you heard wrong. Now, you'll have to excuse us, Rawlings. My wife and I are going to head across the lake. Like I said, we're still on our honeymoon. We've got better things to do than talk business with you."

Without a backward glance, Owen steered Angie out of the café. He said nothing as he guided her to the dock where the launch was tied. He handed her into the boat and leaped lightly in behind her. Then he fired the engine and shoved the throttle forward.

A moment later the launch was tearing across the lake toward the island. Aware of Owen's dangerous mood, Angie sat in thoughtful silence. Her hair flew in the wind. She pushed a lock absently behind her ear as she reran the scene with Jack Rawlings in her mind.

Halfway across the lake Owen eased back the throttle. The roar of the engine faded to a murmur and the launch continued toward the island at a much slower speed.

Owen turned his head to look at Angie. "All right, what the hell was going on back there?"

"Just what you thought was going on. Rawlings wanted inside information on the merger." Angie watched him warily.

"I know that. What I want to know is how you came to be with him in that café. How did you get across the lake?"

"Actually," said Angie, "that's a rather interesting story, now that I think about it."

"Yeah, I'll just bet it is."

"Rawlings sent a kid in a boat over to the island to tell me that someone who worked for my brother wanted to talk to me."

Owen's hand tightened on the wheel. "I should have knocked his teeth down his throat."

"The kid said that Rawlings had tried to call me but couldn't get through to me on the phone." Angie studied Owen's hard profile. "Is that true?"

"No. No one's called." Owen was concentrating on the approach to the island.

"Are you sure, Owen?"

His head came around abruptly; his eyes were as hard and challenging as those of a hawk. "Are you accusing me of lying again?"

Angie shook her head slowly, watching him. She remembered his pride and his promise to her. "No. You told me you would never lie to me. I believe you."

Some of the anger faded from his gaze. "Good. I guess we've made some progress, at any rate. I ought to be grateful for small favors. Damn, Angie, you should never have fallen for that trick. Your father and brother were right when they said you're too naive when it comes to business."

That infuriated Angie. "I am not naive. If people would just take the trouble to keep me informed, I wouldn't fall for any tricks. But nobody bothers to keep me posted, do they? You all keep me in the dark and then get angry when I blunder around on my own or come to a false conclusion."

"Blundering around is exactly what you're doing. You should have used your common sense with Rawlings. You should have known there was something wrong when some jerk sent a message saying he worked for your brother."

"Stop chewing me out, Owen. I reacted in a perfectly normal and reasonable manner, given the circumstances."

"Just what were the circumstances?"

"The guy said he'd been trying to get hold of me on the phone, and I knew you had ordered Betty to direct all phone calls to you. For my own good, of course. Because I'm so naive and all."

Owen glared at her. "Calm down, Angie. You're getting emotional."

"I can't help it. That's the way I am, remember? Furthermore, I do not appreciate being called on the carpet like an employee who screwed up."

"You did screw up," Owen insisted.

"It wasn't my fault."

"It was your fault." He turned and scowled, his feet braced against the gentle motion of the launch. He leveled a finger at her. "You should have known better than to get into some stranger's boat. You should have been suspicious of the message in the first place. You should have waited until I returned before you went rushing off to see what was going on. You should have used a little common sense, damn it."

"You're just mad because you're afraid I might have said something that will hurt the stock offering," Angie muttered.

"Wrong. I don't give a damn about the stock offering right now. I'm mad because that jerk, Rawlings, was trying to use you and you let him trick you into doing exactly what he wanted."

Angie lifted her chin. "I think we had better postpone this discussion until you're in a more reasonable frame of mind."

"Reasonable? You expect me to be reasonable about this?"

"Yes."

"Well, think again, lady." Owen shoved the throttle forward. The engine roared. "We'll finish this conversation later," he yelled above the noise. "You're right about one thing—this is not a good time to talk. At the rate things are going, I might decide to let you swim back to the island."

WHEN THEY ARRIVED Owen was still feeling irritated. But at least he was in full control of his temper once more. As he tied the launch up at the small island dock he thought about how incredibly easy it was for Angie to transform his moods. Around her he could go from rational, deliberate and calm to a state of complete masculine outrage in the blink of an eye.

Discovering Angie in that café with Rawlings had been the final straw. All morning, he had been restlessly mulling over Angie's refusal to admit she loved him. It was a childishly transparent attempt to manipulate him. He'd told himself the best way to handle the situation was to pretend to ignore it. He was sure his reasoning was correct. Angie was too soft and emotional to hold out for long. Sooner or later, she was going to forget herself when she lay in his arms. She would say the words he wanted to hear. And when she did, Owen could tell himself he had won the small, silent battle.

"Owen?"

"Yeah?" He glanced up from where he was coiling a yellow nylon line. Angie was climbing out of the boat, a thoughtful look on her face.

"How did you know I was in that café with Rawlings?"

Owen's hands stilled on the line. Then he stood up and reached out to grasp her arm to steady her. "A kid at the marina said you had gone into the place to meet someone."

"That would be Dave, I suppose."

"Right. Dave." Owen eyed her as she stood in front of him on the dock. "And?"

"I just wondered."

He put his hands on his hips and studied her. "What exactly did you wonder about, Angie?"

"Well, to be perfectly honest, it occurred to me that the timing of this little incident was rather interesting," Angie said slowly.

"Go on."

She frowned. "Okay, look at it this way. You leave the island in your launch and within a short while I get a message that someone representing my brother is trying to get in touch with me."

"Rawlings could have been watching the island with a pair of field glasses. As soon as he saw the launch leave, he probably sent the kid with the message. He knew it was the only way to get you alone."

"True." Angie nibbled on her lower lip, considering that angle. "He referred to what he called the gossip on the street."

"Gossip about what? The old feud?"

"Yes. He seemed to think it was far from settled, and he said that was what worried his investors. They thought it could make for trouble in the new management lineup."

Owen shrugged. "If they're that nervous, they can pass on the offering. I'm not worried about losing Rawlings's group. I checked with my headquarters this morning. The business world is eating up the story of our marriage and the merger. Believe me, there's plenty of interest in Sutherland and Townsend stock."

"That's not my point, Owen."

"What is your point?"

She looked up at him with serious eyes. "On our wedding night someone deliberately tried to drive a wedge between us by making certain I saw an advance copy of the press release about the merger."

"Did a damn good job of it, too," Owen grumbled. "Every time I think about spending my wedding night with a pillow between me and my bride, I get mad as hell all over again."

"That's very touching," Angie said dryly, "but you're still missing my point."

He folded his arms. "So tell me your point."

"The point is that it's obvious someone is still trying to hurt the merger, Owen. Don't you think you'd better find out who it is?"

"You think I haven't been looking?" he asked softly.

"Well?" She tilted her head to one side. "Have you got any ideas?"

He unfolded his arms and shoved his hands into his back pockets. "None I want to talk about yet."

"Why don't you want to talk about them?"

"Because I'm not sure of anything yet, all right?" He heard the irritation in his voice and forced himself to relax.

"You're afraid that one of your relatives is behind this, aren't you? You're afraid this is a family thing."

For a second, he was tempted to deny it. But Angie was watching him with those clear turquoise eyes, and he knew she had intuitively arrived at the conclusion he had reached by dint of painful logic. "Yes. Damn it to hell, yes."

Angie touched his arm gently. "It's all right, you know. You don't have to defend any of them to me. I'm family now, too, remember?"

He looked at her. "I hadn't thought of it that way."

She smiled slightly, her eyes warm. "Don't try to shelter me or keep me out of this. We can deal with it together, Owen. I'm your wife."

"It doesn't feel solid yet," he told her.

"What doesn't feel solid?"

"You and me," he admitted. "I've got a legal document that says you're my wife. I've got my ring on your finger. I've taken you to bed. But something's still missing."

"What more do you want?" she asked.

"I don't know."

Angie's brows rose. Then she smiled. "Let me know when you do figure it out. In the meantime, try treating me like a wife. Let me help you handle this mess."

He wanted to argue. Wanted to demand that she admit she loved him—that she was his as completely as she had been before their botched wedding night at the hotel. But he could not think of how to force the issue while standing on the stupid dock.

He would wait, Owen promised himself. He would wait until he got Angie into bed that night. Maybe then he'd figure out how to get things right between them. He seemed to be able to communicate very well with Angie in bed.

"Owen?"

"There's nothing to handle," Owen said coolly. "Not yet, at any rate." He took her arm and started walking along the dock.

"Owen, please don't shut me out. This is my problem, too."

"It's business, Angie."

"No, it's not. It's family. You know it is."

Owen groaned, sensing that he was not going to be able to deflect her and no longer certain he wanted to. He understood business things. He did not understand family things.

But Angie did.

"I'm used to handling stuff like this alone," Owen warned her warily.

"I know. But you're not alone anymore. You've got me, remember?"

He smiled slowly. "How could I forget?"

"Right. As you once said, we're stuck with each other. I think we should put together all the facts that we've got and see where we're at," Angie said.

Owen thought about it. "The problem is, we don't have a lot of facts. But I've had a feeling all along that whoever's causing the trouble is probably a member of my own warm and loving family. No one else would stand to gain from disrupting the merger."

"No one in the family stands to gain from disrupting it, either," Angie pointed out. "At least, not financially. Everyone will be better off if the stock offering is successful."

"True." Owen glanced at her. "But I think it's obvious that whoever's trying to hurt the offering has something besides a financial goal in mind."

Angie nodded. "Someone is trying to keep the feud alive. Someone would rather lose the potential profits of the merger than see Townsends and Sutherlands bury the hatchet."

Owen sighed. "Celia, Derwin or Helen. Got to be one of those three."

"Celia wasn't here thirty years ago."

"No, but you know that old phrase about someone who is more royalist than the king? Celia's made a career out of being a Sutherland. And she's violently loyal to Dad's memory. She may have taken it upon herself to hurt the merger because she knows Dad would have disapproved of it."

"What about your aunt and uncle?"

"I don't know. Like Dad, they always refused to discuss whatever happened thirty years ago."

"Why don't we talk to Betty?"

Owen frowned. "Betty?"

"She was working for your family then, wasn't she?"

"I think she'd just started. But I doubt she would have been aware of what was happening in the family's inner circle."

"You'd be surprised at what the hired help knows about what goes on in the inner circle. Let's talk to her."

Owen hesitated briefly then decided there was no harm in trying. "All right."

BETTY REACHED for the whistling kettle. She lifted it off the stove and poured boiling water into a teapot. "Of course I knew something terrible had happened. Nobody talked about it, but everyone went around real tight-lipped for weeks." She looked at Owen as she carried the pot to the table. "Your aunt cried a lot. Your father was furious. Derwin had been seeing a lot of

Helen and was about to get engaged to her. I think he knew what was going on, too. He acted very strangely."

"But you don't know what actually happened?" Owen watched her pour tea for the three of them.

"Just knew it had something to do with business. And that everyone was real mad at anyone with the last name of Townsend." She cocked a brow at Angie. "No offense."

"Her last name is Sutherland now, not Townsend," Owen said. "So you don't have to worry about offending her."

Angie picked up her cup. "Don't pay any attention to him, Betty."

"Right." Betty looked thoughtfully. "You know, it's hard to believe the bad feelings lasted all these years. Never did understand that part. Business deals go sour all the time. I've been around long enough to know that. No one holds grudges for thirty years."

"They do if there was more than business involved," Angie murmured. She looked at Owen. "And we've already decided this isn't a business matter."

"No," Owen agreed, his eyes meeting Angie's. "For someone in this family, it's very personal."

"I wish I could help you," Betty said. "All I know is that the Townsends caused a lot of pain around here thirty years ago. Far as I'm concerned, it's about time the old feud was buried and forgotten."

"It's been buried," Owen said. "But someone hasn't forgotten."

"It will all be over soon," Betty predicted. She gave Owen a meaningful glance. "I always knew you had more common sense than your father. He was a good man in many ways, but you couldn't reason with him when it came to some things. Dealing with Townsends was one of his blind spots."

"I know," said Owen. He gave Angie a crooked smile. "But it's not always easy dealing with Townsends. You've got to have a knack for it."

Angie stuck her tongue out at him. Owen chuckled.

Fifteen minutes later, having learned nothing more than he already knew, Owen took Angie's hand and led her out of the kitchen.

"What now?" she asked as they went down the dark hall.

"I'm not sure. I could summon everyone together and stage a big confrontation scene. Try to force the truth out of someone."

"You could cause a lot of pain if you do things that way."

"I don't give a damn about causing whoever's responsible pain. Not after what happened this afternoon."

Angie glanced at him. "What made this afternoon's incident worse than any of the others?"

Owen came to a halt in the middle of the hall. He clamped his fingers around her shoulders. "Don't you realize what happened today?"

Angie wrinkled her brow. "Of course. Someone obviously told Rawlings that our marriage was a fraud. One more attempt to hurt the stock offering."

He groaned at her naïveté. "That was only part of it. What someone was really trying to do was drive another wedge between us, Angie. You and me."

"What are you talking about?"

"Don't you understand? Someone wanted me to see you talking to Rawlings. You were deliberately set up, Angie. So was Rawlings, which is why I didn't flatten him."

"I don't understand."

"You *are* naive, damn it. Listen, I'll try again. It was no coincidence that I was told you were in that café with Rawlings. Someone wanted me to think you were selling inside information to him—maybe arranging a deal on the stock. Someone wanted to prove to me that even after all these years, nothing had changed. A Townsend cannot be trusted."

Angie eyes widened in shock. Then outrage flashed in the turquoise depths. "Of all the nerve," she sputtered. "Of all the sneaky, low-down, rotten *nerve.* A set up. I was supposed to look like a traitor."

"Right. Now you've got the whole picture," Owen said. He could not restrain a small, rueful grin. "And you wonder why us big, bad male chauvinists consider you a trifle naive?"

"But I was innocent," she raged.

"Hell, I knew that," he said impatiently.

Angie blinked. And then she started to grin. A wonderfully smug, utterly feminine grin.

"So you did," Angie said.

10

OWEN EYED ANGIE COOLLY. "What's so damn funny?"

"Nothing." She smiled with perfect innocence, more certain of his love than she had been since their wedding day. Euphoria welled inside her.

"Angie, I am not in the mood for any cute games," Owen warned.

"Yes, dear."

He gave her a small shake. "Why are you grinning like a Cheshire cat?"

"Because I have reached a perfectly logical conclusion," she said smugly. "You'll be pleased to know that I have arrived at this conclusion without any excess of emotion and without so much as a trace of unreliable female intuition or wishful thinking. Just cold, clear logic. Your kind of thinking, Owen. Just the facts and nothing but the facts."

"Angie, what the hell are you talking about?"

"Mind you," she said, "I was fairly certain of this conclusion before I arrived at it through sheer, brilliant logic. But I knew you'd be pleased that I got at it your way as well as mine."

"Damn it, Angie, if you don't tell me what this is all about, I'm going to—"

"Of course I will tell you what this is all about. You love me."

He gave her an utterly blank stare. "Huh?"

"I said you love me. You just proved it."

"I did?"

"Certainly." She smiled at him and put her arms around his neck. "You admit you walked into that restaurant this afternoon, saw me with Jack Rawlings in what could only be called a compromising situation, and you never believed for a moment that I was going to ruin the stock offering by telling him our marriage was a fraud."

Owen's eyes started to harden. "You may not have been screwing up the offering, but you were sure as hell guilty of a number of other offenses."

"Ha! Name one."

"Impulsiveness, lack of common sense and a failure to think about consequences. Most of all, you displayed an annoying tendency to act on your own without consulting your husband."

"You weren't around."

"You should have waited until I was around!" Owen bellowed.

At that moment, Derwin stepped into the hall, frowning in deep concern. "Is something wrong out here?"

"No," said Angie. She smiled beatifically at him.

"No." Owen scowled at his uncle. "This is a private matter."

Derwin nodded, looking grave. "I understand. Sorry to interrupt. I take it you were able to keep your appointment at the marina this afternoon, Angie?"

Angie looked at Derwin and suddenly saw the eagerness in his eyes. The happiness she had been experiencing a moment earlier faded. "Yes, thank you, Derwin."

Owen shook Angie off him and turned toward his uncle. "How did you know about Angie's meeting at the marina?"

Derwin gave Owen a surprised look. "Oh, didn't she tell you? I happened to be taking a walk at the same time as that young man, Dave, arrived with the message that someone wanted to see Angie."

"Is that right?" Owen did not move.

"Yes, of course. I saw her off at the dock myself, didn't I, Angie?"

"Yes, you did." Angie reached out and caught Owen's hand. He resisted, starting to free his fingers. She felt the new tension in him and deliberately squeezed hard. He apparently got the message because his hand relaxed in hers.

"I thought I saw you bringing Angie across the lake awhile ago," Derwin said, pining Owen with a sharp gaze.

Owen's smile was cool. "So you did," he said easily. "I found her having coffee with Jack Rawlings in the marina café. You may have heard of him. Rawlings heads up a group of investors who want a block of Sutherland and Townsend stock when it goes public."

"I see." Derwin's narrowed eyes skipped between Angie and Owen. "Rather odd, isn't it?"

"Not really." Owen swung Angie's hand gently. "But definitely unethical. Rawlings sent her a message saying he worked for her brother. Naturally Angie went flying off to see what it was all about. But she realized soon enough she'd been tricked. Rawlings wanted to pump her for some inside information. She told him to get lost. Didn't you, Angie?"

"Of course."

Derwin scowled at Owen. "And you believed her?"

"Sure," Owen said. "She's my wife. Why wouldn't I believe her?"

Derwin's gaze turned stormy. "She's a Townsend, that's why. But it's obvious you're too besotted to notice what's in front of your very eyes." He stalked off without another word.

Angie felt the stillness in Owen. She looked at him. He was gazing after his uncle, his expression grim.

"Owen?"

"Let's get out of this damn hall."

He tugged her into the study and closed the door. Angie sat down and watched anxiously as Owen sprawled in the big chair behind the desk.

"I don't think you should jump to conclusions, Owen."

"It's Derwin who's behind all this. Got to be." Owen contemplated the view outside the window. "He's bitter because he's been kept out of the management of Sutherland Hotels since the beginning. He's been angry for years—and now he's furious with me because I haven't given him a position, either."

"You don't know it's him, Owen."

"I know it."

"How?"

Owen slanted her a derisive glance. "You saw him a few minutes ago. He thought we were quarreling because I'd found you talking to Rawlings."

"We *were* quarreling because of that."

"Yeah, but I hadn't jumped to the conclusion Derwin expected. I was just mad because you'd let yourself get fooled into seeing Rawlings. I never thought you'd set up a deal with the bastard. But Derwin looked like he just couldn't wait to hear me say you'd sold out the Sutherlands. He set up that meeting, Angie."

"And the other incidents? The fax I received on our wedding night? The telephone call telling me you were planning to divorce me as soon as the stock offering was made?"

Owen nodded grimly. "All of it."

Angie spread her hands. "But how? He's been here at Jade Lake for weeks. You know he has. And you said yourself the whole merger thing was a state secret. No one knew about it except you and my parents and Harry."

Owen's eyes rested thoughtfully on the computer that sat on his desk. "These days you don't always need spies inside someone's company to find out what's going on. Not if you know how to handle a computer. Derwin never had to step outside this house to learn what was going on or to arrange any of those incidents."

Angie followed his gaze. "You think he did it through this computer?"

"Watch." Owen leaned forward and punched a few keys. Then he sat back and waited as the screen flickered to life. "In this day and age all you need is a computer and a telephone. I should have thought of this a long time ago. It's the obvious answer."

Angie got up and came around the desk. She studied the series of memos that were appearing on the screen. "What are those?"

"I kept the merger information out of the computer until the last week of negotiations for security reasons," Owen explained. "Then, right before the wedding, I had to let the vice president of my public relations department know what was going on so he could make the announcement and handle the press. But once Calhoun had his instructions, the secret was vulnerable."

"Because he started writing memos and press releases on the computer?"

"Right. I knew there was a possibility the information would be leaked to the financial community. Hell, the rumors were already circulating because of our engagement. Remember those reporters waiting for us by the limo on our wedding day?"

"Very clearly," Angie said dryly.

"Your father and brother and I had been seen together enough to generate talk. I wasn't worried about the gossip. Rumors can be useful in a situation like this."

"Why?"

"They heighten the sense of excitement in the investment community. Palmer, Harry and I figured they wouldn't hurt so long as . . ." Owen broke off, frowning darkly.

"So long as I didn't hear them?" Angie concluded sweetly.

"You weren't likely to hear them during the week before the wedding," Owen said. "You had your hands full with wedding preparations. And according to Palmer and Harry, you never paid much attention to the business, anyway."

"My interests have certainly broadened lately, haven't they?"

"Very funny," he growled. "The point is, this computer—plus Derwin's fondness for tinkering with gadgets—explains how he knew what was going on. He's obviously taught himself how to use the computer to access Sutherland files."

"What about the fax?"

"Easy to send a fax with this setup." Owen drummed his fingers on the desk. "Once he knew the fax had been delivered, he simply picked up the phone and dialed our room at the hotel." Owen's hand clenched into a fist. "My own uncle."

"All right," Angie said quietly. "We know how it *could* have happened. But we still don't know why."

"I told you why. Derwin's been resentful and angry for years because Dad never trusted him with a major role in Sutherland."

"But he has a vested interest in Sutherland Hotels, just as everyone else in this family does. Why would he jeopardize the stock offering? There's a lot of money at stake."

Owen shrugged. "He's had years to nurse his grudge."

"I think there's more to it than that, Owen." Angie was silent for a moment, thinking. "It's got something to do with the old feud, not just Derwin's grudge against your father. Betty said that it wasn't just another business deal that went sour."

Owen scowled. "It doesn't matter why Derwin's so bitter. It's enough that we know he had a motive and—" he nodded toward the computer "—opportunity."

"So did everyone else around here. In fact, up until you offered your brother-in-law a job, your sister and Celia had motives, too. Even your aunt is resentful toward the Townsends. And they all had access to the computer at one time or another. Kim and Glen could have used a computer while they were in Hawaii."

"Aunt Helen knows nothing about computers. She's not into gadgets the way Derwin is. Neither is Celia or Kim. Glen could have managed the job, but I don't think he did. He had no reason to sabotage the merger."

Angie watched Owen's face. "What are you going to do?"

Owen was quiet for a moment, obviously considering his options. "Confront Derwin. Tell him I know what's going on. Tell him that it stops right now or I cut off his income and Helen's, too."

"There might be a better way of handling it, Owen." She perched on the edge of his desk.

Owen swung around to face her. "Yeah? What do you suggest?"

"I think you should find out exactly why your uncle did what he did. Then maybe you should consider doing things a little differently than your father did them. Would it hurt to give Derwin a seat on the new board of Sutherland and Townsend?"

Owen's mouth dropped open. He recovered himself immediately. "Are you crazy?"

"Owen, think about it, please. You could handle him if he tried to stir up trouble. But my guess is he wouldn't be a problem. I think he'd back you in any move you made."

"I don't believe this. First I have to offer Glen Langley a job and now Derwin. Angie, quit trying to tell me how to run my company and my family!"

"I've got a stake in both. Why should I keep my mouth shut?"

"Because you don't know what the hell you're talking about."

Owen got to his feet. "I don't want to hear another word of advice, is that clear? I'll make my own decisions around here."

"You know, while we're on the subject, you really should think about deeding this house over to Celia. Apparently she feels your father had promised to leave it to her. And it's not as if you want the place. You hate it."

"Deed the house over to Celia? Good God, you don't know when to stop, do you?"

"Just a thought, Owen." She smiled her most winning smile.

"*Stop thinking,* damn it."

"Yes, Owen."

"I mean it, Angie. Don't think I haven't realized how you've been trying to manipulate me lately."

"That's not true." She stared at him, appalled. "I haven't been trying to manipulate you."

"Come off it, Angie."

"It's true. I've simply made a couple of suggestions, which you have wisely considered, that's all. I know very well I couldn't possibly manipulate you into doing anything you didn't want to do, Owen. Nobody could."

His eyes narrowed. He leaned back and beckoned with one finger.

"Come here, Angie," he ordered softly.

Wary of the new gleam in his eyes, she eased off the desk and took a step toward him. "Why? What do you want?"

"Come here and I'll tell you."

"I don't like the look in your eye, Owen Sutherland."

"Come here, Angie."

"Not unless you tell me what you have in mind."

"Come here, Mrs. Sutherland." Owen's voice deepened, becoming as smooth and rich as honey. His eyes held hers as surely as if he had reached out and caught hold of her wrist.

A rush of sensual excitement seized Angie. She sensed the desire in him and it drew her like a magnet. She risked another step forward and smiled.

Owen's hand clamped gently around her wrist. He stood, drew her against his chest and pinned her there, one palm curved around her buttocks. Deliberately he spread his legs so that she stood between his thighs.

"Well?" Angie demanded in a voice that trembled with anticipation. "What do you want, Owen?"

"Tell me you love me." His hand slid to her nape.

The request surprised her. It was not quite what she had been expecting. Angie hesitated. "Why should I tell you that? You don't care about love."

"I want to hear you say the words." He brushed his mouth lightly across hers, silently urging her to comply. "You haven't said them since our wedding day."

"I haven't had a good reason to say them." She twined her arms around his neck, vitally aware of the heat and strength in him.

"You do now." He kissed her brow, then the tip of her nose.

Angie shivered as the liquid warmth coiled inside her. "I don't see why I should. You haven't said those words to me."

"We're talking about you, Angie. Not me." He tightened his thighs around her hips, anchoring her. Then he started to slowly undo the buttons of her shirt. "We'll see who can manipulate whom around here."

"Owen, this is not fair."

"I've decided I want to hear you tell me you love me."

"Why?"

"I like it." He parted her shirt and slipped his hand inside to cup her breast.

"Owen, wait . . ."

"Tell me, Angie." He skimmed his mouth down her throat, pushed aside her collar and kissed her bare shoulder.

"Owen, stop. What are you trying to do?" Angie struggled briefly as she realized he was going to put her through sweet torture until she capitulated.

"Say the words, Angie." His hand dropped to the waistband of her jeans.

Angie heard the snap and the sound of her zipper being lowered. She was trembling, her body sensitized and aware. She breathed quickly, trying to steady herself. "Wait. Let's talk about this. I know you're annoyed because you think I've been trying to manipulate you. But I swear, it wasn't like that, Owen."

"Tell me you love me, Angie." He slid his hand inside her panties.

She gasped. "All right, maybe I was trying to pressure you a little bit. But I wasn't trying to manipulate you. I was just trying to give you some guidance. I wanted you to think about your feelings. I just wanted you to realize how you really felt about me, Owen."

"Say it, Angie." His fingers curled against her, seeking her softness. He nuzzled her neck.

"Look at it from my point of view, Owen. You've obviously got a problem admitting your deepest feelings to yourself, let alone to others. But I know your emotions run... *Oh.*"

"Do you love me, Angie?"

"Owen, stop! Anyone could walk in on us."

"If anyone does, he or she will turn right around and walk out again." He withdrew his hand, then slid his leg between hers and pushed at her gently with his thigh. "Love me, Angie?"

So much for trying to pressure him into admitting he loved her, Angie thought. When it came to this kind of resistance, he had a lot more stamina than she did. Owen was a pro at standing up to pressure.

"I love you, damn it." Angie gripped Owen's head between her hands and kissed him with a surge of exasperation and enthusiasm. "I love you, I love you, I love you. And you love me, Owen Sutherland. Admit it."

He ignored her passionate demand. Instead, his mouth closed roughly over hers, searing her lips. The masculine hunger in him enveloped Angie, drawing her into the heart of the storm. Owen's need for her was all-consuming.

And so was his love, she told herself as he lifted her and carried her across the room to the couch. *If he could only bring himself to admit it.*

The door of the study opened without any warning. Helen walked into the room. "Owen? Owen, what is going on? I just talked to Derwin. He tells me you found Angie with someone named Rawlings and that you . . . oh, my God."

Angie was flat on her back on the couch. She groaned and closed her eyes, making a quick grab at her parted shirt. Owen, one knee on the couch, turned to glare at his aunt.

"Excuse me," Helen said coldly. She made no move to leave the room. She stood there, glaring with anger and disapproval.

Owen straightened slowly, a resigned look in his eyes. Keeping himself strategically placed between Angie and his aunt, he confronted Helen. "What seems to be the problem here?"

Helen braced herself defiantly. "I demand to know what is going on."

Owen ran his fingers through his hair, a gesture Angie had come to learn indicated disgust. "Well, since you ask, I was about to make love to my wife. Any objections?"

Helen's face went red and her lips thinned. "I do not particularly care about your ill-mannered personal behavior at the moment. Has Angie been giving inside information about Sutherland to this Rawlings person?"

"No." Owen shoved his shirttails inside his jeans and slanted an amused glance at Helen. "Do you think I'd be making love to her if I'd just caught her in the act of selling me out?"

"Who knows what you would do? It's obvious she's seduced you," Helen said tightly. "Derwin's right. You're just a puppet on her string. I've warned you before about the way Townsends go about deceiving people. But you won't listen, will you? You never listen to anyone. You think you know everything." Helen's eyes glistened with tears.

"Helen . . ." Owen started toward her.

"Go back to your cheap little seductress of a wife. Go on. You'll find out what Townsends are really like." Helen turned and fled. The door slammed behind her.

Silence descended on the study. Angie sat up cautiously, all trace of passion gone. She was silent for a long moment. "Owen, there's more to this than we know. More than just Derwin's bitterness over not being allowed to work at Sutherland. Your aunt's anger is too passionate, and it's all directed at my family."

Owen was staring at the closed door. "You think she was involved in whatever happened thirty years ago?"

"I'm not sure what to think." Angie stood. "All I know is that we've got to find out what happened before we take any further steps."

"Celia?" Owen cocked his brow inquiringly.

"I don't think she'll be able to help us any more than Betty could. But we can try."

"The hell with it," Owen said. He finished adjusting his clothing and strode to the door. "I'm going to get everyone together in one room and we're going to have this out once and for all."

"Owen, wait." Angie fumbled with her clothing and ran after him. "I'm not sure that would be a good idea."

"I'm not particularly interested in your analysis of the situation," Owen called over his shoulder as he went down the hall. "I want some answers and I want them now. Go find Celia. Tell her I want her in the living room in five minutes."

"But, Owen—"

"Just do it, Angie."

Angie trailed to a halt. Maybe he was right. Maybe it was time to force the issue. Assuming Owen could get everyone to talk. "All right."

TEN MINUTES LATER Angie sat tensely on the sofa near the window. She watched the expressions on the faces of her new relatives as Owen let the silence hang heavily in the room.

The emotions ran the gamut. There was anxiety and concern on Celia's patrician features. Derwin and Helen sat rigidly upright in their chairs, their expressions reflecting bitterness and something that might have been fear.

Owen stood at the window looking implacable and completely controlled. Angie wondered if this was the way he was when he called a meeting of his board of directors. She was suddenly rather glad she did not work for him.

Owen let the seconds tick past while he gazed over the lake. Night was falling rapidly. Lights were winking into existence on the far shore. Jade Lake was quickly turning from dark green to black.

He finally turned slowly to face the others. "I've had enough of this nonsense about the old Sutherland-Townsend feud. I know full well that certain recent incidents aimed at causing trouble between Angie and me have all been caused by someone in this house."

Derwin looked offended. "How dare you accuse us?"

"Believe me, once the facts are set out, it's damned easy to accuse you." Owen met his uncle's gaze. "Only a fool could miss the pattern. The Townsends are innocent."

"I wouldn't be too sure of that, if I were you," Derwin muttered.

"Derwin," Owen said with cold patience, "I know *how* things were accomplished and I know *when* they were accomplished. I am fully aware that the computer in my study was used. The only thing I don't know for certain is why someone here is so determined to ruin this deal with Townsend. Would you care to tell me?"

"I don't know what you're talking about," Derwin snapped, his gaze focused on the lake outside the window.

"I'm talking about what happened thirty years ago."

Helen straightened her shoulders. "Why don't you try asking the Townsends?"

"I did," Owen said quietly. "Palmer Townsend says he does not know what went wrong thirty years ago, and I believe him. All he knows is that the deal to merge the two companies went sour at the last minute and that my father would never speak to him again."

Derwin narrowed his eyes. "Palmer Townsend knows what went wrong. Hell, he was the cause of the trouble."

Angie was incensed. "That's not true."

Owen threw her a repressive look. "Quiet, Angie. We're going to get to the bottom of this. This is no time for an impassioned defense of your family. Save the emotion for later."

"If you think I'm going to sit here and let your uncle slander my father, you're out of your mind," Angie shot back furiously.

"What I think," Owen said very softly, "is that you should sit there quietly while I sort this out. The last thing I need right now is a display of Townsend theatrics."

He was right and Angie knew it. She subsided, contenting herself with a glare.

Owen turned to his uncle. "Derwin, I think we'll start with you. Tell me what happened thirty years ago."

"I don't see why I should be forced to dredge up the past," Derwin argued.

"Put it this way," Owen said in a softly menacing tone, "either you tell me what happened or you and Helen can dredge up a new source of income."

Derwin stared at him, clearly shaken. "Are you threatening to cut us off from Helen's share of the Sutherland income?"

Angie groaned and closed her eyes briefly. The others looked at Owen in disbelief and outraged shock. Owen took no notice.

"Now you're starting to understand, Derwin. Talk."

Derwin drew himself up stiffly. "Very well, if you insist. But you aren't going to like what you hear."

"Just talk, Derwin."

Derwin glanced at Helen then faced Owen. "It's quite simple. Townsend never intended a genuine merger. What was intended was a hostile takeover of Sutherland Hotels. When it was over Sutherland would have been effectively swallowed up by Townsend Resorts and all of us would have been out in the cold."

"Try another story, Derwin," Owen suggested.

"It's true, I tell you," Derwin sputtered. "Your father found out that Townsend had been quietly buying up shares of Sutherland stock through a third party. Once he had acquired enough stock, Palmer Townsend could have forced the merger on his own terms. He almost succeeded. But your father realized what was going on in time to stop it. It cost Sutherland Hotels a fortune because we had to buy back a lot of the company stock. It was tough going for a while, but we did it."

"My brother managed to forestall the hostile takeover," Helen put in. "Just barely. He made two decisions after that. One was to make certain that Sutherland Hotels never lost controlling interest in its own stock again. The second decision was never to trust a Townsend."

Owen shook his head in disgust. "That is a bunch of crap. Don't expect me to buy any of it."

Celia frowned. "How do you know that, Owen?"

"Because out of curiosity I took a look at the stockholder records from thirty years ago. My father was no fool. He always made certain he held at least fifty-one percent of the stock. He was never vulnerable to a hostile takeover. But something did change his mind about the merger with Townsend, and I want to know what it was."

"Are you saying I'm lying about what happened thirty years ago?" Derwin demanded.

"Yes," Owen said. "I am. The question is why?"

There was an appalled silence. Unable to meet anyone's eyes because of the pain she was afraid she would see, Angie focused on the view outside the window. She noticed a small speedboat roaring toward the island. She frowned, studying the three figures in it closely.

"Owen?" she said tentatively.

"Not now, Angie."

"I think we've got company," Angie said.

"What are you talking about?" Owen turned to follow her glance.

The small boat cut its engine as it neared the island. It closed in rapidly on the small dock. The lights of the boat house revealed the familiar face of the man who leaped out of the boat. The two other people in the craft piled out and started moving swiftly up the path.

The lights from the terrace gleamed on Harry Townsend's red hair and the set, determined faces of Angie's mother and father.

"Well, hell," Owen muttered. "Just what I needed. A landing party of Townsends coming to rescue Angie from a fate worse than death. You know something? This really is the last straw."

11

"I'LL GET THE DOOR," Owen told Betty as he stalked into the hall. "Looks like we'll need a couple of extra places set at dinner and two more bedrooms made up for to-night. My in-laws have arrived unexpectedly."

Betty grinned, wiping her hands on her apron. "Well, well, well. This should be interesting."

"If I were you, I'd stay in the kitchen until the fur stops flying."

"Think I'll do just that. You can handle this, Owen. You've got a wife who will help you."

Owen opened the door and found himself confront-ing an irate father-in-law, a furious brother-in-law and a worried mother-in-law.

"What a pleasant surprise," Owen murmured. "We were just talking about you Townsends."

"I demand an explanation, Sutherland," Palmer Townsend said before he was even through the door.

Harry pushed past Owen, searching the hall. "Where's Angie? What the hell is going on here, Suth-erland? We got a message this morning that you've got her stashed here until after the stock offering. Some jerk claims you're going to divorce her as soon as the stock goes public."

"Some jerk lied," Owen said calmly. "Come on in, Marian," he said to Angie's mother. "You look as if you've had a long trip."

"You would not believe what I've been through today." Marian smiled uncertainly. "Palmer and Harry went crazy when the message came this morning. We flew to San Francisco and rented a car to drive up here. We've been hours on that winding road trying to find Jade Lake. Neither Palmer nor Harry would stop for directions. It's been incredible."

"You're just in time for dinner," Owen said.

Angie came into the hall. She smiled brightly. "Hi, everyone. What's all the excitement about?"

"Typical Townsend reaction to a family crisis, dear," Marian said. "Everyone is going bonkers."

"I am not going bonkers," Palmer snapped, looking ferocious. "And neither is Harry. But we do want some explanations, by God."

"You'll get them." Owen put his arm possessively around Angie's shoulders. She stepped close, signaling her loyalty in no uncertain terms.

Palmer and Harry did not miss the small but highly significant action. Harry glared at his sister. "Are you sure you're okay, Angie?"

"I'm fine, thank you."

Palmer looked at Owen. "Just what the devil is going on around here? I thought you two were heading to a Sutherland hotel for your honeymoon."

"So did I. Our plans changed." Owen led the way to the living room, his arm still firmly around Angie. "Have a seat, everyone. I'll make the introductions for those of you who don't know each other personally. Then we're going to finish hashing this out."

"I don't see what needs to be hashed out," Palmer muttered. "All I want is an explanation." He nodded brusquely to Helen, his face softening slightly. "Hello, Helen. Been awhile. Almost didn't recognize you."

"Hello, Palmer," Helen said softly.

Owen caught the brief, odd look on his aunt's face as she greeted Palmer Townsend. He studied her more closely out of the corner of his eye while he ran through the introductions. Owen realized Angie was covertly watching his aunt, too.

"When this is all over," Owen concluded, "we're going to have dinner and go to bed. In the morning Angie and I will be leaving to finish our honeymoon at an unspecified Sutherland hotel."

Angie gave him an amused, interested look. "We will?"

"Yes, we definitely will. Now, let's get on with this miserable business." Owen decided to take a chance. "Helen, I think it's your turn."

Helen looked stunned. "But I don't have anything to say about what happened all those years ago. There's been enough damage done. Owen, can't you let things be?"

"No," Owen said deliberately gentling his voice. "I can't."

Derwin spoke up angrily. "What happened thirty years ago has nothing to do with you, Owen. You were just a child."

"You're wrong, Derwin. Whatever happened then is affecting my marriage and my business. This mess has got to be cleared up now. Let's get one thing straight, here. No one is leaving this island until I have the truth." Owen looked at his aunt again. "Helen?"

Derwin leaped to his feet. "Stop badgering her. The least you could do is show some respect for your own aunt, Owen Sutherland. She's your father's sister, after all."

Owen felt Angie's fingers slip gently into his. She squeezed his hand reassuringly, and he knew she was telling him to continue on his present course. "I'm sorry, Helen. But I have to have some answers."

"I know," Helen whispered. "I always knew that sooner or later it would all come out." She burst into tears.

Derwin hurried over to her, thrusting a handkerchief into her hands. "You don't have to tell him a thing, Helen."

She blew her nose and shook her head firmly. "No, Owen's right. This has gone far enough. We've lived with this all these years and I, for one, am tired of it."

Palmer eyed her closely. "This has something to do with me, doesn't it, Helen?"

"Yes. Yes, it does. I'm sorry, Palmer."

Owen saw Marian glance at Angie and raise her brows, but she said nothing.

"All right, Helen," Owen said gently. "Tell us what happened."

"What happened," Helen said, her voice firming as she spoke, "was that I made a foolish mistake thirty years ago. My only excuse is that I was rather young. And somewhat sheltered. And accustomed to being spoiled, I suppose. To put it in straightforward terms,

I fell in love with Palmer Townsend the minute I saw him. And, with typical Sutherland arrogance, I convinced myself that he was in love with me."

Owen shot a quick glance at his in-laws. Palmer looked unhappy and uncomfortable. Marian appeared sympathetic. Harry looked surprised.

"There was a great deal of excitement in the air because of the plans for a merger between Sutherland and Townsend," Helen continued. "Everyone was bubbling over with enthusiasm, full of anticipation for the future. I decided nothing could be more romantic than Palmer and I marrying and uniting the companies and the families through a fairy-tale wedding."

"Helen, you don't have to say any more." Derwin gripped her shoulder.

"He's right, Helen. Don't pay any attention to Owen, here," Palmer said. "This is personal. You don't have to spill your secrets to all of us."

She smiled sadly. "But I do. Owen is right. They aren't just my secrets. They affected all of us in one way or another. The rest of what happened is quite simple. I went to Palmer and told him that I was in love with him and that I wanted to get married. He was startled, to say the least. Stunned would be a more apt description."

Palmer looked at the toes of his shoes. He was turning red.

Helen continued with an apologetic smile. "He tried to be a gentleman and let me down easy. But when I realized he was not in love with me and, indeed, had never considered me more than a casual friend, that he was about to become engaged to someone I had never met, I became enraged. I did something very wrong. Something I have regretted for thirty years."

"Helen, that's enough," Derwin said. He patted her shoulder—an awkward but tender gesture.

"No, not quite." She touched his hand briefly, her eyes going from Palmer to Owen. "In a jealous rage, I became determined to ruin the merger. I'm the one who gave inside information to certain financial backers. It caused them to change their minds about loaning money to the company that would have been formed by the merger. Those same backers later decided to finance some Townsend expansion plans. My brother naturally assumed that had been Palmer Townsend's scheme from the beginning."

There was a collective gasp around the room. Owen leaned forward and propped his elbows on his knees. He frowned thoughtfully. "What was the information, Helen, and how did you get it?"

Helen shrugged. "Just some accounting data about one of the resorts in the Sutherland chain that was having difficulties. I got the information from a secretary. It wasn't difficult. I had heard my brother talking about the situation and knew he wanted to keep it quiet until after the merger. When I sent the information anonymously to the financial backers, I implied that the troubled resort was only one of many. They believed it. You know how gossip affects business deals."

Palmer looked at Owen. "I remember that problem resort. Bad location. Your father planned to sell it off and that's what he eventually did. It never really hurt the rest of the chain."

Helen looked at her folded hands. "My brother was furious when the backers mysteriously pulled out of the deal and turned around and financed Townsend. He was sure a secret deal had been made."

"He thought I'd convinced them that Townsend was a better bet on its own than a Sutherland-Townsend merger," Palmer said slowly. "He decided I'd changed my mind about the merger and used inside information to get the backers to drop their interest in Sutherland and get behind Townsend, instead."

Helen nodded. "My brother turned the company upside down looking for your spy. He eventually came to me. When he pinned me down, I told him another lie."

Palmer looked at her, his eyes narrowed slightly. "You told him I had seduced you in order to get inside information, didn't you?"

"Yes," Helen admitted. "I think my brother could have forgiven a few shady business maneuvers on the part of a competitor. But I knew he'd never forgive you for what I told him you did."

"And that's why he hated my guts all those years." Palmer shook his head in wonder. "Well, at least now I understand why he took such a dislike to me after the deal fell through. But why didn't he confront me?"

"I begged him not to. I told him my pride was at stake. He understood."

"Sutherland pride," Owen muttered ruefully.

Angie smiled at him. "I always knew there was a lot of passion in this family. All kinds of passion."

Owen tightened his grip on her hand. "So much for the cool Sutherlands." He glanced at Helen. "Was I wrong about Derwin being behind all the recent incidents, then? Was it you?"

"No," Derwin answered quietly. "You were right. I was the one who tried to cause enough mischief to ruin the stock offering. I found out about the merger and the marriage too late to head either off, but I thought if the stock didn't do well, you and Townsend might undo the merger and go back to running the corporations separately. It was a long shot, but it was all I could manage on such short notice. I had to try."

Palmer stared at him in exasperation. "For God's sake, man, why? We're all going to make a lot of money out of this merger."

"Some things are more important than money," Derwin said proudly. "I had to try to protect Helen from the pain I knew she would experience if Sutherland and Townsend eventually got together on a permanent basis. I knew what had happened thirty years ago, you see. I knew how passionately she had once loved you, Palmer. I detested you for having caused her so much unhappiness, even though it eventually paved the way for me to become engaged to her."

Palmer frowned at him a moment longer then nodded. "Sure, I can understand that."

Harry shrugged in sympathy. "Yeah. I can see where you'd feel you had to try something now, Derwin."

"Perfectly reasonable of you, Derwin," Marian murmured. "And I certainly understand why you did what you did, Helen. Unrequited love can be dreadfully painful. One can do foolish things because of it."

"It was all a bit drastic," Celia observed. "But I suppose one can understand."

"Absolutely," Angie said. "Poor Helen. How perfectly awful it must have been for you. And it was wonderfully loyal of you to try to protect her from having to confront my father and be humiliated this time around, Derwin."

Helen smiled sadly at Derwin. "The thing is, it was only a matter of pride, not love. I realized that soon enough when I discovered it was Derwin I truly cared for. But I was afraid to confess the truth afterward. It would have been so humiliating and it was too late to repair the damage, anyway. I was hoping everything would be forgotten. But it never was."

Owen scanned the faces of everyone in the room. He groaned and dropped his head into his hands. "Somebody save me from all this *emotion*. Even my father fell victim to it. I cannot believe I am surrounded by people who seem to have no problem at all understanding thirty years of business decisions based on smoldering vengeance and unrequited love. *Thirty years.*"

"Now, Owen," Angie said, patting his shoulder sympathetically. "You're overdramatizing the situation, dear. It's not that bad."

He raised his head and glared at her. "Not that bad? Are you crazy? Its absolutely incredible that either corporation has survived this long with such emotional people in charge. How the hell are we going to run the new Sutherland and Townsend with a board made up of seething, passionate overreactive people like this?"

Everyone in the room turned to stare at him. Owen glowered. Angie smiled gloriously.

"You're going to put some of your family on the board?" Palmer asked, looking interested.

"Why not?" Owen said. "You, as president, and I, as chief executive officer, each get to appoint an equal number of board members, right?"

"Right?"

"You're no doubt going to put Harry on as soon as possible."

"Sure. And my wife. I like to know I've got people I can count on behind me when I get into a fight," Palmer said.

"Yeah? Well, I want people *I* can count on to back me up when you and I get into it, Palmer." Owen looked at his uncle. "I could use the kind of loyalty you've shown to Aunt Helen for thirty years, Derwin. What about it? Will you take a seat on the new board?"

Derwin looked startled then flustered, his surprise obvious. "Well, I... Yes. Yes, of course. Be glad to help out on the new board." He stood a little straighter and beamed proudly at his wife.

"And what about you, Celia?" Owen switched his gaze to his stepmother. "If you're on the board you can look after Kim's interests in the company. There will probably be grandchildren one of these days, too. You'll want to protect their futures."

"I'm deeply honored, Owen." Celia studied him closely. "But I don't really know much about running a business like Sutherland and Townsend."

"Something tells me you'll learn fast. And I already know you're loyal to Sutherland interests. That counts for a lot. By the way, while we're on the subject of grandchildren, I want you to know you can have this house for them. It's all yours. I know Dad would have wanted it that way. He just didn't bother to spell it out in the will. You know how Dad did things."

"He expected you to take care of everything. Yes." Celia smiled slowly and nodded. "Thank you, Owen. Thank you very much. And I accept the seat on the board."

Owen turned to Helen with a questioning glance.

"No, thank you," Helen said gently. "I don't need a place on your new board of directors. I trust you and the others to look after the family interests. And I'd really rather spend my time with my charity projects, if you don't mind."

Owen nodded, appreciating the quiet vote of confidence. "Thanks."

"Hey, what about me?" Angie bounced up and down and waved her hand eagerly to get Owen's attention. "I'd like to be on the new board of directors. I'll take the seat Helen doesn't want. It'll be great fun. I've got all sorts of really terrific ideas for the company, including a new logo."

Owen heard Palmer and Harry groan. He ignored them as he turned to his bright-eyed wife. He decided to try logic first. "You've already got a career designing jewelry, remember?"

"Yes, but I'm sure I could manage two careers," she said quickly.

"Angie, honey, you and everyone else will own shares in the new company. That will give you some say in how things are run. You don't need a seat on the board."

"But, Owen—"

"For crying out loud," Owen exploded, abandoning logic, "you're sleeping with the CEO. How much more clout do you want?"

"It isn't the same," she insisted, blushing furiously as everyone grinned. "Give me a shot at it, okay, Owen? I just know I'd make a great member of the board. I'll attend every meeting and I'll volunteer for special committees and everything."

"I'll just bet you would." Owen grinned slowly. "I'll be real blunt, Angie. I'm going to love you for the rest of my life and then some, but it will be a cold day in Hades before I allow you onto the board of directors of Sutherland and Townsend. Something tells me you're going to cause more than enough trouble just holding a few shares of stock."

"Owen." Angie's lips parted in astonishment. Her eyes widened with delight. "What did you just say?"

"You heard me."

"Owen, you *do* love me. I knew it."

Owen barely had time to brace himself as Angie hurtled straight into his arms.

"Oomph," Owen muttered, his arms going around her immediately.

She clung to him, smothering him with kisses as the assembled majority stockholders of Sutherland and Townsend cheered.

Betty walked into the living room and took in the scene of Sutherlands and Townsends laughing uproariously together. She caught Owen's eye over the top of Angie's head and smiled broadly.

"Always knew there wasn't anything wrong around here that couldn't be fixed up with the love of a good woman. Now, then, dinner is served. I just can't wait to see all you Sutherlands and Townsends sitting down to a meal together."

THE FOLLOWING EVENING Angie stood on the terrace of the honeymoon suite of a familiar Sutherland hotel. The evening breeze rippled the silk of her silver peignoir. She leaned her elbows on the railing and watched the sunset far out over the Pacific. Her long, silver earrings swung gently.

Mentally she began designing a graceful, curving bracelet of beaten silver that would capture and reflect the colors of twilight. She would start sketching again soon, she decided. She had only been away from her jewelry design work for a couple of weeks, but she was already starting to miss it. Her art was a part of her, and when she was away from it for very long she got a little restless.

She turned as she heard the door of the suite open behind her. Owen walked in carrying a bottle of champagne and two glasses in one hand. He was wearing the black dinner jacket, pleated white shirt and black trousers he had worn to dinner.

He paused long enough to close the door and lock it securely. Then his gaze skimmed over the elegant white and silver room until he saw Angie out on the terrace. He started toward her and began to loosen his black bow tie. His smile was slow and warm and full of sensual promise.

Angie shivered under that warm gaze as if Owen had touched her. She watched him stalk across the white carpet like a jungle cat, moving with sleek power and masculine grace. She saw the love and the hunger in his eyes and she thought again how much she loved him.

Owen came to a halt near her. He put the bottle and glasses on the white wrought-iron table. He opened the champagne with a few smooth, efficient movements. Then he poured two glasses and handed one to Angie. He lifted his own in salute.

"To you, Mrs. Sutherland."

"To you, Mr. Sutherland."

Owen waited until Angie had taken a sip of the bubbling champagne. Then he removed the glass from her hand and put it on the table beside his.

Very deliberately he reached around her waist to grip the wrought-iron railing behind her. He looked at her as she stood gently caged in front of him.

"Now, then, Mrs. Sutherland." He kissed her slowly, taking his time, letting her feel the endless need and love inside him.

Angie smiled and twined her arms around his neck. "Yes, Mr. Sutherland?"

"I believe," Owen said, his lips on her throat, "that you and I still have some unfinished business."

"Is that right?" She trembled under his lingering, compelling kisses. She tipped her head back and let her hair tumble over her shoulders. "And what would that be?"

"A wedding night."

"Ah. That." She laughed up at him with her eyes and started to unfasten his white shirt. "Do we need to call a meeting of the board in order to get approval of this merger, or do you think we can manage it on our own?"

"The board of directors of Sutherland and Townsend has already given this its full approval. I think we can handle the details just fine all by ourselves." Owen's mouth came down on hers. He scooped her up in his arms. He strode into the white and silver room with her and put her on the bed.

When Angie looked at him she saw that he was watching her silver gown slide around her thighs. She smiled at the look in his eyes, reached up and took hold of the ends of his tie. She tugged gently.

Owen laughed huskily as he allowed himself to be pulled down onto the bed. He lay sprawled on top of her and threaded his fingers through her hair in a now wonderfully familiar gesture.

"Tell me you love me, Angie."

"I love you, Owen. I shall love you all of my life." She touched the strong line of his jaw with gentle fingertips.

"Just as well, because I am going to keep you close for the rest of our lives, come what may." He caught her hand and kissed the golden band on her finger. "I love you, wife. Forever."

"Forever."

TEN MONTHS LATER Owen paused outside a hospital room door. He was carrying a dozen red roses in one arm and a large manila envelope in the other. He did not bother to conceal his proud grin as he walked into the room. The place was littered with gifts from various members of the Sutherland and Townsend clans. Pink ribbons and brightly colored wrapping paper lay everywhere.

Angie looked up from the infant in her arms. She smiled, her eyes glowing with love and happiness. She looked tired, Owen thought with some concern. But he had to admit he had never seen anything so beautiful as the sight of his wife holding their baby.

Angie looked at the flowers. "Owen, they're lovely. What's in the envelope?"

"The kid's first share of Sutherland and Townsend stock." Owen opened the envelope and removed the stock certificate made out to Samantha Helen Sutherland. "Think she'll like it?"

Angie laughed. "She's going to love it when she graduates from high school, that's for sure. At the rate the stock is climbing these days, she'll be able to finance law or medical school with her share."

"Maybe she'll decide to be the next CEO of Sutherland and Townsend." Owen leaned down to admire his baby. The infant did not open her eyes, but her tiny hand closed tightly around his thumb. Owen laughed at the strength and determination in that small grip. "She knows how to hang on to what she wants."

"Just like her father," Angie agreed.

"Right," said Owen. He looked at Angie. "And I am never going to let go of you, Mrs. Sutherland. Remember that."

"I will," Angie said. And she smiled at him the way she had on her wedding day when he had put his ring on her finger.

The way she would for the rest of their lives.